**"I WANT YOU, AMANDA. I HAVE NEVER
WANTED ANY
WOMAN BUT YOU...."**

"I never wanted a divorce and before we leave this
place, you're going to tell me why you insist on
getting one."

"I thought—I *think*—it's for the ... best," Amanda stammered, avoiding his probing stare.

"Best for you? Or me? Amanda, you can't arbitrarily decide something like that."

"You don't understand."

"You're right. And I'll never understand if you
won't talk to me. Tell me what happened to us. Tell
me why having a baby changed everything in our
lives."

"There's no point, Dain. You could never understand."

"But I do understand this...." His mouth found
hers and she knew the die was cast. She was going to belong to him—again—physically, if in no
other way. His arms went around her, drawing her
against him, ignoring her resistance as if it weren't
there. . . .

CANDLELIGHT ECSTASY ROMANCES ®

GOLDEN VOWS

Karen Whittenburg

A CANDLELIGHT ECSTASY ROMANCE ®

Published by
Dell Publishing Co., Inc.
1 Dag Hammarskjold Plaza
New York, New York 10017

Dell ® TM 681510, Dell Publishing Co., Inc.
Candlelight Ecstasy Romance®, 1,203,540, is a registered
trademark of Dell Publishing Co., Inc., New York, New
York.

ISBN: 0-440-13093-X

Printed in the United States of America
First printing—July 1984

For my parents, with love

To Our Readers:

We have been delighted with your enthusiastic response to Candlelight Ecstasy Romances®, and we thank you for the interest you have shown in this exciting series.

In the upcoming months we will continue to present the distinctive sensuous love stories you have come to expect only from Ecstasy. We look forward to bringing you many more books from your favorite authors and also the very finest work from new authors of contemporary romantic fiction.

As always, we are striving to present the unique, absorbing love stories that you enjoy most—books that are more than ordinary romance.

Your suggestions and comments are always welcome. Please write to us at the address below.

Sincerely,

The Editors
Candlelight Romances
1 Dag Hammarskjold Plaza
New York, New York 10017

CHAPTER ONE

Even in the clutter of noise around her, Amanda heard him laugh. That rich, throaty, baritone laugh that still made her heart catch and teased her lips to smile. She looked up from arranging the trays of hors d'oeuvres, her gaze skimming over the faces of her guests to find him.

Dain Maxwell stood by the fireplace, as he always did at these parties. It was his favorite spot in the entire house, and he insisted it was her duty as hostess to circulate while he kept the party alive in the corner.

He seemed to be doing a good job of that tonight, she thought. The group around him was obviously entranced with what Dain was saying. He lifted his hand to emphasize a point and Amanda focused her attention on the lithe movement.

She'd always been fascinated by his hands. Large, graceful hands that symbolized so much of the man. Hands that could sketch the intricate details of an idea and create a skyscraper; then, with the same consummate skill, those hands could trace the contours of her body and create pleasure.

She followed his movements as he absently rubbed the back of his neck. He needed a haircut, Amanda noted. The thick, wheat-gold hair at his nape touched the collar of his black evening jacket with sharp contrast.

In many ways, she thought, Dain was her contrast. Her features were delicately feminine, sketched with a subtle reserve and inherent privacy that contrasted with the ready warmth of her smile. The rugged lines of his face held a refinement usually lacking in such masculine features, a certain hint of gentle strength that contrasted with the latent power of his body, a body that contrasted with hers in the most intimate of ways. The texture of his skin was like rough velvet against her own satin softness and it was as if her curves had been designed to conform to his shape.

His hair was the color of sunlight, hers was dark as midnight. His eyes were a rich, earthy brown while hers were as blue as a sapphire sky. He stayed tan all year because of the hours he spent in the sun, but her complexion remained creamy no matter how much time she spent outdoors.

Dain was determination; she was acquiescence.

Her gaze lowered to his wide shoulders and she admired the smooth fit of the evening clothes and his virile physique that complemented them. Dain was careful about keeping in shape. Although he never said much about it, it was obvious in his enjoyment of vigorous activities, in the way he lobbed a tennis ball across the court or swam the length of the pool. It was obvious in the way he hoisted the sails of the sloop and then sat back to breathe deeply of the salt-scented air.

Amanda had often thought Dain was a throwback to the ancestors whose name he bore, had even teased him about the Viking warrior stance he affected at times. But she'd always loved that particular trait, envied his ability to square his shoulders and face life with intrepid challenge.

If only she could possess a measure of his courage. . . .

Amanda let the useless thought crumble as she watched him conclude the story he'd been relating. The group around him broke into laughter and again she heard the husky tones of his amusement. He glanced in her direction and, suddenly, she was trapped by his eyes, held motionless as the laughter died on his lips and his smile faded into the restless curve of his mouth.

Amanda looked down at the display of food on the table before her, but all she could see was the dark indifference of his eyes. Indifference. It was time she faced facts and stopped crediting Dain with feelings he didn't have. The lack of emotion in his expression didn't stem from acceptance of what had happened. He simply didn't care.

"Another successful May Day celebration, Amanda."

At the sound of the feminine voice beside her, Amanda busily finished rearranging the trays, then with a casual smile she turned to her guest. "Thank you, Meg. I couldn't have managed without your help."

"Oh, come on, Amanda. You don't have to be the gracious hostess to me. I'm painfully aware of the help I haven't been this year." Meg laughed easily. "But my own guilty relief that I don't have to clean up when the party is over eases the pain somewhat. At least, all of our friends know better than to accept an invitation to our house."

With a disbelieving shake of her head, Amanda ran a

quizzical gaze over Meg's slender, picture-perfect appearance. It was hard to believe that a woman who could manage five, boisterous sons and a husband who always seemed to be searching for his glasses could panic at the thought of giving a party.

"You don't fool me," Amanda said, absently brushing at the short tendrils of hair at her temple. "I've enjoyed some memorable evenings at your home."

"Of course they're memorable, Amanda. Just like old *I Love Lucy* reruns." Meg's amused tone of voice belied her serious expression. "For example, I'm sure you remember the party I gave when you and Dain returned from your honeymoon. I mixed the date with little Jerry's birthday party and the caterer delivered one hundred and fifty ice-cream clowns instead of the finger sandwiches I thought I'd ordered. You have to admit that was a party no one will soon forget."

Amanda couldn't help laughing and her eyes sought Dain's in an impulsive wish to share the memory, but he wasn't looking at her. And even if he had been, she thought he probably no longer remembered.

With a practiced smile that concealed her thoughts, she turned her attention back to Meg. "It was a wonderful party, Meg. And besides, just think of all the stories you'll be able to tell your grandchildren someday."

"God forbid! I absolutely refuse to be a grandmother! It's bad enough being a mother—" She stopped abruptly and Amanda saw the sudden apology that shadowed Meg's eyes. "Oh, Amanda, I didn't mean—"

"You don't have to explain," Amanda interrupted, deliberately misunderstanding in order to keep the conversation from an uncomfortable subject. "I know you wouldn't change one single thing about your life, even if you could."

"No. No, I wouldn't." A frown of indecision creased the lovely lines of Meg's face. "Amanda, I . . ." She paused, obviously searching for the right words. "I know I've told you this before, but I really am sorry about the baby. You've done so well these past six months that I almost forget sometimes how hard it must—"

Amanda touched Meg's arm in a not-too-subtle hint, knowing she couldn't endure another expression of sympathy, not even from Meg. "If you don't mind, Meg, would you go over and keep Tom Coleman company? It looks like his wife has left him to fend for himself while she flirts with my husband. Good thing Dain isn't susceptible to redheads, isn't it?"

"Dain has never been susceptible to any woman except you," Meg commented, her voice resuming its former light tone as she looked toward Dain's corner of the room, then back to Amanda. "You're really very lucky, you know."

Amanda nodded her agreement and watched her friend cross the room. As she smoothed the satin sheen of her dark evening dress, her gaze drifted slowly, inevitably, back to Dain. Lucky. Meg had meant the words to convey comfort, but they settled in Amanda's heart with ominous weight.

Lucky Mandy, Dain used to tease her. Lucky at cards, lucky at love. How many times had he told her she'd been lucky to marry him in a weak moment when his resistance was low? But his eyes had always betrayed the lie to his teasing, telling her that he'd been the lucky one.

The sun always shines for you, Amanda, he'd said in more serious moments. *Share it with me.*

Someone jostled against her and the memory of Dain's words slipped behind a polite exchange of small talk, only to resurface as soon as the guest left her side. She stared thoughtfully at Dain, watching him with a familiar ache of emptiness as she remembered the days of sunshine. She had believed in luck in those days, believed that the dreams they shared were destined for reality.

With a bittersweet smile she remembered how lucky she'd felt the first time he'd asked her for a date. As a full-time college student and part-time apprentice in interior design at the architectural firm where he worked, she had admired him from afar. Young, ambitious, and with a charming resistance to feminine lures, Dain had been the fairy-tale fantasy of most of the women in the building. An elusive man who kept his thoughts and feelings to himself.

His quiet self-sufficiency had been a challenge Amanda accepted with youthful confidence. The first overtures of friendship had been hers, but gradually she grew to depend on him, on his understanding, his tenderness, and the easy curve of his smile. She had lost her heart to that smile, and when he proposed she'd felt incredibly, wondrously lucky.

But luck was now a memory. Dain no longer smiled and the sun didn't shine for her anymore.

As if conscious of her regard, Dain shifted and, even if it was unintentional, effectively turned his back to her. With a sigh Amanda checked the contents of the ice bucket, lifted it in her arms, and started toward the kitchen, pausing now and then to speak with the people she passed.

Alone for the first time during the evening, Amanda leaned against the kitchen's center island and let her composure relax. She eased the arch of one slim brow with her fingertip, grateful that for a few minutes at least, she didn't have to smile. It was becoming too much of a habit to hide her thoughts and feelings behind that mask. Too easy to assume the role of perfect hostess, wife, or friend, depending upon the situation. She must stop the emotionless masquerade soon, before she lost the ability to distinguish reality from the image she projected.

Lucky Amanda. She would have liked to tell her friends that she wasn't lucky at all. It was a lie. A lie that concealed the empty core of her failure. A lie that allowed her to pretend nothing had changed, that Dain still loved her.

But she couldn't lie to herself. Her marriage had been over for some time now. All that remained was for her to admit it. Dain was waiting for her to make the first move. She sensed it in the careful way he watched her and in the way he chose every word he said to her. So why was she waiting?

Pressing her palms hard against the woodblock counter, Amanda let her gaze wander over the room. Shiny copper pans hung in a gleaming row along the wall. A red-brick fireplace curved out from the corner, its black, swing-out kettle a reminder of cooking's humble beginnings. The fireplace had been Dain's idea, his contribution to the modern kitchen, which was supposed to have been her sole responsibility to design.

"You'll love it, Amanda," he'd promised her as he'd ruthlessly sketched his idea onto the houseplans, rearranging her own careful drawings to make room. "Just think of all the marshmallows you can burn to a crisp . . . right in the comfort of our kitchen."

She had been unimpressed until the room took shape and she had seen how the fireplace added a homey touch. On the day they'd moved into the house, Dain had presented her with a moving day gift—an extra-long metal skewer with a wooden handle, carved with the words MANDY'S MOLTEN MARSHMALLOWS.

Amanda closed her eyes and could almost hear the sounds of her long-ago laughter blending with Dain's. An echo of the sheer joy she'd felt just in loving him.

Pivoting abruptly, she carried the ice bucket to the refrigerator and methodically began to refill it with ice. This kind of longing would get her nowhere. Dain, who had once been friend, companion, and lover, had become a stranger, a constant reminder of all she'd had . . . and lost.

She didn't know how it happened or when, only that it had. For weeks after the baby died she'd lived in a void. Everything existed on a superficial level and she had survived each day simply because nothing could penetrate her outer composure. But now the memories were pushing against her wall of defense from the inside, creating a pressure that would crush her if she didn't yield.

And yielding meant she must face facts and make decisions. Decisions like moving from this house with all its reminders of once-upon-a-time. Decisions like leaving Dain.

Her hand trembled at the thought, but Amanda forced it to stop. She had accepted the death of her child and she would learn to accept the death of her marriage. It wasn't fair to continue a relationship that offered so little to both of them. She wanted more than a man who stayed with her out of a sense of responsibility. She deserved better and, in all honesty, so did Dain. Circumstances had irrevocably changed her from the carefree, innocent girl with whom Dain had once fallen in love. Even if she thought there

18

might be a chance to regain his love, she couldn't be that person again.

It was over. For better or for worse.

"Is everything all right?"

Slowly Amanda turned to face her husband. Dain stood just inside the doorway and she had the sudden impression that he'd been there for some time. Odd, she thought. Once she would have known the instant he'd entered the room, no matter how many people were around, and now they were completely alone, only a few feet apart, and she hadn't even realized he was so near.

The seconds passed in cool silence as she looked at him. As if painting a portrait, her gaze stroked every familiar line in his face, even the tiny scar beside his left eyebrow. One day soon she wouldn't be able to look up and see him standing in the doorway, but her memory would hold his image and save it for a time when it was no longer painful to recall.

"Everything is all right," she answered, knowing it was both the truth and a lie.

Dain nodded and his lips formed that polite, plastic smile that she hated. "I should have known better than to ask. You always have everything under control, don't you, Amanda?"

For the first time in months she didn't force herself to match his artificial expression. The indifference in his voice hurt and she was tired of pretending to herself that it didn't. "Is there a problem?" she asked. "I just came in here to get some ice."

"The Hendersons are leaving now. I thought you'd want to say good night."

"Of course." Amanda replaced the lid of the ice bucket and handed it to Dain. "Would you mind?"

19

He took the container from her hands and followed her from the room. For a split-second as she walked through the doorway she wondered how he would react if she turned and flung herself into his arms. She frowned at the ridiculous idea, knowing that more than likely he would drop the ice bucket in astonishment and then, in that awful, polite voice, he'd ask if she wanted him to get more ice.

"Oh, there you are, Amanda," Terri Henderson called from the entryway. "We have to leave, but I wanted to tell you what a lovely evening we've had. May Day Revels. What a good idea for a party. Thanks so much for inviting us. See you soon." The brunette walked to the front door, but her husband lingered to touch Amanda's hand.

"You're a charming hostess, Amanda," he said. "I hope you and that lucky husband of yours throw a party every spring for years to come." With a wink he squeezed her hand and then followed his wife from the house.

Spring. The one word stayed in her mind as Amanda returned to her guests. *Spring.* The season of beginnings. A year ago she'd carried the beginning of a new life inside her, a precious secret shared only with Dain. Why hadn't she realized then that beginnings also meant endings? Why had she ignored the warning signs and convinced herself that Dain was as happy as she?

"Great party, Amanda." Another guest touched her arm before leaving.

She hoped she made the proper response, but the thoughts persisted and made her only vaguely conscious of saying good night to the departing guests.

Spring. This year she carried the challenge to make a new beginning with her life. And next year? Maybe next year, if she were lucky, someone would invite her to join

20

in the May Day festivities. Next year the beginnings and the endings would be over. Everything would be all right again.

As she closed the front door for the last time, Amanda sagged against its solid oak strength for a minute before pushing upright and walking into the living room. Dain had taken off his jacket and loosened his tie, but he still stood beside the rock fireplace. He glanced up when she entered the room and then resumed his pensive study of the hearth. Amanda made a visual survey of the party's aftereffects, the full ashtrays, the empty wineglasses scattered around the room, the table almost bereft of food. An aura of gaiety still lingered in the air like a concerto's final chord, faint and fading.

Without conscious intent, Amanda began to restore order. For her, the ritual of cleaning was as much a part of the party as the preparations. It helped her relax and unwind. Tonight, though, it seemed mechanical, just something to occupy her hands while she waited.

"Thank you, Amanda. I think everyone had a good time. I know I did."

It was what he always said after a party but, somehow, hearing him say the expected words helped ease her tension.

"I noticed what a good time you had," she said, her voice searching for the light, teasing tone that had once come so naturally. "You seemed to keep the guests in your corner entertained."

Dain watched her as she moved quietly about the room, his expression unrevealing, but oddly restless. "I don't know why we bothered to hire a cleaning woman. You never leave anything for her to do."

He always said that, too, at the end of a party.

"I'm only straightening things up." She repeated her standard answer and expected it to echo in the cavern of emptiness between them. Dear God! When had they grown so far apart that they couldn't think of anything original to say to each other?

Amanda stopped in mid-motion and set the ashtray down without emptying it. "Dain, I—" She faltered, not knowing how to form the right words. But as she met his eyes she knew there weren't any right words. There was only one way to say it and Amanda gathered her courage. "Dain, I'm leaving you."

Like a pebble dropped into a pool, her words fell between them and she felt the shock ripple through her to collect in her throat. In a matter of seconds she wished she hadn't said it, wished she had said it differently, wished there wasn't a reason to say it at all and, finally, repeated it. "I'm leaving you."

For one shattering second, thick lashes shadowed his expression, but he gave no indication of surprise. "Leaving me," he said in a stiff, impassive voice. "Does this mean we're getting a divorce?"

Somehow Amanda kept from flinching at the word. *Divorce.* Leave it to Dain to put a name to this aching nonentity within her. "I . . . yes." She almost strangled on the admission before she steadied. "Yes, I guess that is what I mean."

"You guess?" The corner of his mouth lifted with incisive question. "Haven't you already seen an attorney?"

An attorney. A nameless authority who would draw up legal documents to sever their relationship in a few strokes of black ink. Amanda blanched at the prospect. "No, Dain . . . no, I hadn't even thought about contacting an attorney."

"You'll have to do that, Amanda. That is the first step in getting a divorce, you know. You hire an attorney to represent you. Then you discuss the settlement with him. Who gets the house, who gets the car, that sort of thing. Your attorney will draw up a petition for the court and send me a copy, which I will then discuss with my attorney. If I agree to the settlement, bingo, we have a quiet, agreeable divorce. If I disagree, we'll battle about it in court and a judge will decide how to disburse our joint possessions."

Amanda was appalled at his emotionless recital. How could he be so calm, so matter-of-fact? She wanted him to drop the impersonal tone and tell her how he really felt . . . or was he telling her in the cool indifference of the words? "Dain, I . . . I'd—"

"Oh, and you'll need to state your reasons for wanting a divorce." He shrugged slightly. "A mere formality, of course, but the law requires that you have grounds. Would I be too inquisitive if I asked what grounds you plan to give, Amanda?"

"Grounds?" she echoed stupidly.

"Why, Amanda?" He rubbed his jaw impatiently. "Why do you want a divorce?"

She looked away from his enigmatic gaze and then forced herself to look back. She knew why, but how could she tell him? It was the silence, the stilted silence between two people who had shared love and commitment and who now had nothing to say. They had lost the ability, the reason, to communicate with each other and it seemed ironic that he should even ask her to explain why.

Dain raked his fingers through his hair and then released an audible breath. "Would you like me to list some possibilities?" he asked, the words heavily under-

23

lined with his exasperation. "You might try incompatibility. I believe that's often given as grounds for divorce. Or perhaps, in our case, it should be 'irreconcilable differences.' "

"Don't, Dain," she protested. "Don't make this difficult."

"Do you find this difficult, Amanda? It doesn't have to be." An odd sort of hesitancy crept into his voice. "We could try talking about other alternatives if you like."

Her thoughts hit the idea and skittered away. Didn't he realize that there were no alternatives? He didn't love her anymore. Any lingering doubts she might have harbored had vanished at his practical acceptance of her decision. No, there were no alternatives.

She lifted her chin in hopes it would bolster her resolve. "Talking won't change anything."

"It might. Maybe we should consider a separation. It would give you a little more time to sort things out."

Separation? A slow, agonizing uncertainty? She couldn't do that. Dain had already given her time to "sort things out." It wasn't fair to play on his sense of responsibility for her. "I—I think it's best my way," she stated flatly.

His lips pressed together in an emotionless smile. "All right, Amanda. We'll do it your way. When do you plan to make this momentous move?"

She stiffened at the bitter edge in his words and drew her pride around her like a cloak. "I don't know. Is it important? I—I guess I can leave any time you want me to."

Dain narrowed his eyes in sudden piercing anger. "God, I could wring your lovely neck for that, Amanda. That and about a thousand other things!" He turned and his hand hit the rock of the fireplace with a resounding slap. The subsequent silence vibrated against the walls and beat mercilessly in her ears.

A tremor began at her nape and worked downward, leaving her shaky and unsure of herself. She wondered at his unexpected anger. Did he feel guilty because he'd stopped loving her? Was there some underlying resentment that they had to have this confrontation at all? Dain hated arguments and he always avoided them. . . .

Always. She must stop thinking of him that way. *Always* and *forever* didn't exist for herself and Dain anymore. Always was past and forever was only a few days away. Her heart pounded out the seconds, gradually slowing as she focused on his hand.

His fingers splayed over the surface of the rock to form a contrast of light against dark, a parallel between two separate strengths. Dain had pulled each of those stones from the ground himself.

Amanda had lost count of the hours they'd spent searching for rocks of just the right shape and color. Some had come away from their mother earth with little or no persuasion, but others had resisted Dain's efforts to uproot them.

She had been amazed and touched by his determination and, where she would have given up and chosen a different stone, Dain had worked tirelessly to get the one he wanted. And now all the stones were welded into a wall of conjunctive strength, much like the wall of hidden emotions that separated her from Dain.

"When, Amanda?" He spoke without turning toward her, his voice muffled by the fireplace.

"Soon," she answered, pulling her attention to the reality at hand. "A few days, maybe a week. Does it matter?"

He shook his head and swung to face her. All trace of anger was gone. She saw only the polite concern of a stranger. "You can have the house. I'll find another."

"I can't stay here, Dain. Surely you understand?"

He just looked at her, his eyes reminding her of dark, winter nights. "What are you going to do?"

Amanda hesitated, weighing what she wanted to say. Above all else, she had to be positive he felt no misplaced responsibility for her once she walked out the door. "I don't have any definite plans yet. I suppose a place to live is the first priority and, then, maybe a short vacation. I've always wanted to see what the big attraction is in Texas, you know."

"I remember," he said softly. "We didn't make it that far, did we?"

Memories of shared vacations crowded through her mind. Was she really standing here, talking about taking a trip without him? "I suppose I should talk to an attorney as soon as possible." The composure of her voice astonished her almost as much as the words she said. "Jerry is an attorney. Maybe he would . . ." She paused awkwardly. "But that might not be a good idea, since Meg and I are close friends."

"I'm going to ask Jerry to represent me," Dain put in smoothly, as if it had been decided long ago. "I'll ask him not to discuss the divorce with Meg, if you want."

"Oh, no. I'm sure he'll be diplomatic about the whole thing. I guess I'll find someone else, then . . . to represent me, I mean," Amanda said, and wanted to scream with outrage. They were speaking of divorce, the end of almost six years of caring and touching and loving each other, as if it were no more than a simple errand. All of a sudden she hated him. Hated him for making her fall in love with him, for giving her everything and then taking it away. Hated him because he could stand there without a trace of regret, coolly accepting what she could never accept.

"It's settled then." Strangely enough her voice didn't betray her emotions. "I'll get in touch with an attorney as soon as I've found a place to stay."

"Fine, it's settled."

Amanda met his eyes in reluctant agreement, her vehement reaction dying beneath a flicker of disappointment. The tiny candleflame of hope that he wouldn't allow her to leave was quietly snuffed out.

"I think I'll go to bed." She walked to the doorway, wondering if she should tell him she was sorry or that she had truly loved him once. But he knew that already, so she just stopped and looked back over her shoulder. "It was a good party, wasn't it, Dain?"

"The best," he answered, feeling his throat constrict painfully as Amanda lifted her chin and walked regally from the room. Dain raked his fingers through his hair before he patted his shirt pockets in search of a cigarette, knowing he wouldn't find one. He hadn't smoked in years, but he needed one now. He needed a drink too.

Action followed the thought and he poured a shot of bourbon into his champagne glass. The liquor burned through the tightness in his throat and he poured himself another, only then realizing how his hand shook.

God! What had she done to him? If she'd stayed another minute, another second, he'd have lost control, maybe even followed through on his threat to wring her neck. His fingers curled tightly around the delicate, crystal glass, then relaxed.

Whom was he trying to kid? If he'd touched her, there would have been no threat. The feel of her smooth skin

27

beneath his hand would have been his undoing and he would have crushed her in his arms and punished her with kisses until she yielded to his will. Once he wouldn't have hesitated. Once he wouldn't have doubted his right to touch her. And once she would have yielded.

He stopped the useless reminiscence. Once was gone. Over. Finished. She was leaving. And he would forget.

Dain took another swallow of his drink and felt his whirling thoughts slow and settle in his mind. It was best this way, he told himself. A divorce. A quick, clean break with the past.

I'm leaving you. The memory of her softly spoken words twisted inside him like a knife blade. But the wound wasn't fresh. Amanda had left him a long time ago. He didn't know when or how or even why, but it had happened. So slowly that he hadn't realized it until too late, she had drawn away from him, shut him out of her life by degrees and left him waiting helplessly for the finale.

He'd been expecting her to do something to change the situation. He'd even been aware of her struggle to reach a decision, but still he felt as if his whole world had collapsed at his feet.

And she had stood there, so calm and composed, with no desire to talk to him or to work things out. She had just stood there, as if leaving him were the easiest thing she would ever do. He hadn't realized until that moment just how far apart they'd grown.

I'm leaving you. Well, he could survive without Amanda.

Dain caught sight of his reflection in the window. The offset lighting gave back a distorted image, and he closed his eyes against what he saw there. But shutting out the visual image only made the inner one more clear.

28

He was afraid. A derisive sound tore from his throat. He, Dain Cameron Maxwell, survivor of all challenges fate had thrown his way, was afraid that he couldn't survive without Amanda.

So why was he letting her leave? The whisper came faint but persistent from his heart. Had he grown so soft that he didn't have the courage to fight for what he wanted?

Dain considered the idea, letting his mind replay again and again the conversation with Amanda. Was it his imagination or had he seen a flicker of disappointment in her eyes tonight? Maybe there was an ember of love for him hiding behind that cool indifference. And if there was . . .

Determination flowed through him in exhilarating waves and the fragile crystal in his hand shattered under the pressure. Dain was hardly aware of the splintering glass, thinking only that he would make her love him again.

"All right, Amanda," he whispered to the silent night. "I'll do things your way . . . for now. If you want a divorce, we'll go through the motions of getting one, but it won't be easy for you. I'll make damn sure it isn't easy."

Picking up a napkin from the table, he dabbed at his hand and studied the rock fireplace. He'd built that wall himself, stone by stone. And if it took every ounce of strength he possessed, he'd tear apart the wall Amanda had built between them. Stone by stone, if necessary, but one way or another, he would win her back.

CHAPTER TWO

The Maryland countryside rolled past the car window in vivid splashes of color as the odometer of Dain's Mercedes clicked off the miles with solemn insistence. Amanda could almost hear the seconds ticking past with the same urgency. Time was spinning crazily forward, rushing her toward the inescapable consequences of her decision.

Amanda glanced sideways at Dain, wondering if he dreaded the next few hours as much as she did. His face was unrevealing, his attention focused on the highway and his hands sure and confident on the steering wheel. If he had any apprehensions, they weren't apparent.

She turned her head and stared out the window, unable to deny her own disquiet. Her mother and father had accepted the news with concern, insisting that Amanda come home to "think things through." But she had refused, knowing that their home was no longer hers and that she couldn't bear their solicitous advice. Dain's parents had offered their standard, uncaring, "We've been expecting something like this to happen" answer.

But Martha. Amanda felt a sigh catch in her throat. Telling Martha would be one of the harder consequences to face. Martha Pemberton had been friend, family, and surrogate mother to Dain since his childhood. Amanda had been surprised and, at first, even a little jealous of his respect and love for the elderly woman. But Martha had soon stolen Amanda's heart as well, and there had never been any doubt about the love that overflowed from Martha to Dain and expanded to include Amanda. Over the years of her marriage Amanda had grown to feel as comfortable with Martha as she did with her own parents and infinitely more comfortable than she had ever felt with Dain's.

Brushing at an imaginary wrinkle in her navy cotton slacks, Amanda frowned. If only Dain had let her come alone. . . . But she knew, as well as he did, that Martha would expect them to face her disapproval together. Even though she herself had never married, Martha was a proponent of marriage, of working to make one last and she wouldn't be reticent about voicing her opinion.

Amanda could imagine the fierce disappointment that would alter Martha's usually amiable expression and roughen her already gruff voice. It was all too easy to imagine the look in Martha's green eyes—a look that said they were naughty children in need of a scolding. And Martha would take it as her right to scold them. But, in the end, she would accept the inevitable and love them both as unconditionally as she always had.

Pressing her lips into a tight line, Amanda focused on the passing landmarks. Divorce. Was there no end to the guilt? She had wrestled with her conscience during the last

31

few days, struggled with the reality of what she'd done. Leaving Dain wasn't a decision she'd reached overnight. It had been building inside her for months, but now that it was almost a fact, she was plagued by doubt. It was the right decision, the only logical thing to do. So why did it feel so wrong?

She glanced at Dain's familiar profile. How had they come to this? When had their love changed from the lighthearted give and take to this heavy feeling that there was nothing left to give? And when had the ordinary quarrels inherent in marriage changed to resentful, angry attacks that undermined the roots of their relationship? And when had the suffocating politeness begun?

Amanda knew she could search her memory for the rest of her life and never pinpoint the beginning. Maybe it had started with the divergent course of their careers. As his architectural designs began to gain an appreciative audience, Dain had spent more and more time at the office and away from her. His business trips came more frequently and always at an inconvenient time for her. Finally he'd stopped asking her to accompany him. She had invested more of her energy in her own career as an interior design consultant, but that hadn't satisfied her longing for a family.

Maybe it had started when they decided to have a baby . . . and couldn't. Maybe it was Dain's gradual forming of new friendships that never really included her. There could be a dozen maybes that sparked the beginning, she thought with a rueful sigh.

Hurried meals, hurried conversations, a life-style that left them little time for each other. It had all spelled trouble, but she had been naively confident that the pace would slow, that they would be able to really communicate again, once they had a child. But when she finally did become pregnant, the respite from tension had been short-lived and nothing seemed to be right between them.

And now, months later, they were traveling a familiar road on their way to face Martha and an impossible explanation of how they had come to this end.

"Only a few more miles." Dain's voice brought her around to meet his eyes.

"Yes," she said as her stomach muscles tightened in protest. How could he be so calm? "Only a few more miles."

She noticed how his gaze lowered to her hands and immediately realized she was twisting her wedding ring back and forth. With a conscious effort she stopped the nervous action and wondered what habit would replace it once she removed the ring.

"Not nervous, are you?" he asked casually.

"Of course not." She paused before tempering her denial with the truth. "At least not any more so than I was the first time you brought me to meet Martha."

"That bad, huh?"

Amanda bit her lower lip and then nodded. "I'm not looking forward to this at all, Dain."

"I'd be disappointed if you were." His lips curved in a sudden smile. "We could always take the shortcut."

"Oh, no. I remember exactly where that shortcut leads," she stated, visualizing a grassy clearing cradled by tall trees and rocked by the gentle lullaby of a nearby brook. If she closed her eyes, Amanda knew it would all come back to her. The sights and smells and sounds of the secluded clearing would all come back as a soft background for the memory of Dain loving her. She kept her eyes determinedly open. "No shortcuts, Dain. We almost didn't make it to Martha's house at all that day."

"But when we did, you weren't nervous anymore."

Amanda couldn't have prevented her fleeting, reminiscent smile even if she'd tried. "No. I wasn't nervous anymore."

Dain studied her thoughtfully. "Martha isn't going to take sides on this, Amanda. Surely you're not worried about that?"

"No. I'm sure she'll be very understanding." Abruptly Amanda turned her gaze to the window. "Understanding! God, I didn't think this would get so complicated."

"No, I'm sure you didn't."

The faintly pious tone of the words irritated her. Dain, of course, would have expected complications. Thrived on them, in fact. And he'd certainly weathered the tension of the past week better than she had.

No. Amanda stopped the accusing thoughts. She knew that wasn't fair. Several times lately she'd noticed definite signs of strain in his face. Tiny lines fanned the corners of his eyes, and the scar had become more evident to her experienced gaze. No. This wasn't easy for him either. But soon it would be over. Soon she'd have a minute to stop, take a deep breath, and gain some much-needed perspective on the new direction of her life. Some insight into the woman she had become during the past year.

The rough motion of the car made her suddenly aware of the new direction of the road. She glanced curiously at Dain.

"Is this the right way to get to the clearing?" he asked, peering inquisitively at the graveled road. "Do you remember, Amanda?"

As if he didn't, she thought. "We'll be late getting to Martha's, Dain. Isn't she expecting us?"

For a second he looked deeply into her eyes and Amanda caught her breath as she had once done whenever he glanced in her direction. Was there a shadow of hurt in his eyes? Or was it simple impatience? She had no way of knowing if she had seen either emotion or if it was just a trick of the sunlight.

"Martha knows we're coming," he said. "But this won't take long. I just want to see if the brook is as peacefully beautiful as I recall."

"It won't be." A shiver of reluctance coursed through her at the thought of finding their special place just as she remembered it. "The clearing has probably been bulldozed into oblivion to make room for a housing addition."

"They wouldn't dare."

His reaction pleased her but, as he guided the Mercedes over the bumpy road, Amanda felt the protest grow inside her. She didn't want to see what had happened since the last time she'd been with Dain at the clearing. If her prophecy was correct, she didn't want to know and if it wasn't . . .

Amanda sighed softly. If it was still the same, lovely spot, she didn't think she could bear to know.

"See? I told you, Amanda." Dain seemed almost jubilant as he slowed the car beside a cluster of tall, leafy sycamore trees. "Not a house in sight. I'm going to make sure the brook is still there too. Do you want to come?"

Yes. Of course she wanted to. "No. I'll wait in the car," she said, hoping he would accept her refusal at face value.

His eyebrows quirked with the merest hint of a challenge. "Somehow I didn't think you would. No point in raking up old memories at this point, is there? It's probably best that you stay here, Amanda. I'll let you know if anything is different." He shut the car door and strode toward the trees without a backward glance.

She frowned as she watched him walk away. Everything would be different because she was different. Dain was different. Some things were best forgotten. And it was just a place after all.

Her fingers hovered uncertainly above the door handle. Just a place, she thought. A place where Dain had asked her to marry him. A place where he'd held her, kissed her, loved her. Just a place.

The door swung open at her touch and she stepped onto the graveled road. She narrowed her eyes at the cluster of trees before starting forward. As her feet followed the barely discernible trail, her wary heart followed the more clearly perceptible path of memory. It had been a long time since she'd thought about that first shortcut into the woods. A long time since she had remembered that mischievous light in Dain's eyes. The light that should have warned her—if she had wanted to be warned.

"Look at this, Amanda," he'd shouted that day, calling her to his side and pointing to the path. "This looks suspicious to me. I think we should investigate."

She had glanced over her shoulder to Dain's old, but treasured Chevrolet and then met his eyes with a lift of her brow. "I thought you said this was a shortcut to Cape St. Claire and that you knew this area like the back of your hand. Don't tell me you don't know where this path leads."

He lifted his right hand in playful solemnity. "On my sacred honor as a gentleman, I swear I do not know where this path will lead."

He reached for her hand and covered it in his. "And if

36

I should be lying, may the ogre of the woods come and carry me away."

"Oh, terrific," Amanda grumbled as she followed him. "And what am I supposed to do when that happens?"

"You might try hysterical screaming, but if that doesn't work you'll have to rescue me. Otherwise, it will be a long walk home. I have the car keys, you know."

"Always planning ahead, aren't you, Dain?" she teased. "Remind me to turn you in to the knight-errantry commission. If you can't behave in a more chivalrous manner and, at the very least, throw the keys to me while you're being carried away, I'm afraid you'll never earn a white charger."

"You're behind the times, Amanda. These days, any knight worth his salt has a white Mercedes. The upkeep on chargers is just too high."

She had smiled at his nonsense and hoped that when he did have that Mercedes, she would be the damsel in distress he chose to rescue.

A bend in the path slowed her steps and the memory faded. Lazy patterns of sunlight filtered down through the thick foliage and Amanda paused to appreciate the green and gold tapestry of spring. It had been spring then, too, she thought, her mind drifting back to that day as she walked on.

Dain had led her to a clearing, surrounded by trees and serenaded by the soothing sounds of water flowing over rocks. Amanda remembered how she had looked for the sound and caught a glimpse of a sheltered brook. Then she had turned to Dain, her fingers impulsively tightening around his. "This is the place you told me about, isn't it? Where you used to come as a boy? Oh, Dain. It's beautiful!"

37

His gaze circled the small clearing with satisfaction. "It is, isn't it? I used to believe there really was an ogre in the woods and it was great adventure to thwart his attempts to catch me and make it here to safety."

"I'm glad he never caught you."

"So am I." Dain brought his gaze to her face, the look in his eyes saying more—so much more—than the words. Somewhere inside her she had known their relationship had reached a turning point. From the moment of their first meeting, Dain had tended to be reserved, sharing only bits and pieces of his past and his plans for the future. But slowly Amanda felt he had come to trust her and now . . .

With an intuition beyond her experience she had recognized what he was sharing with her. It wasn't the place or even the fact that he'd brought her here. It was commitment and the willingness to overcome his natural self-sufficiency and admit that he needed her. A pledge of love and trust that she would want to do the same. Amanda had heard his words in her heart before they ever left his lips.

"Amanda, I love you."

Emotion had constricted her throat as she lifted her hand in acceptance. She didn't know who moved first, whether Dain stepped forward to take her hand or whether she simply followed her heart into his arms. But suddenly she was there, where she'd always wanted to be. His mouth closed over hers, tender and mobile, and she shut her eyes to lock in the exquisite wonder of the moment.

It wasn't the first time he'd made love to her but, as he lowered her unresisting body to the bed of grass, Amanda knew she would always remember this as the first. Her senses were heightened by the natural beauty surrounding them. The sights and fragrances would always color her memory of this place and Dain and the feel of his hands moving over her.

Her fingers memorized the planes of his face and stroked the golden weight of his hair while he freed her breasts from the bondage of blouse and bra to glory in his caress. Amanda arched her back, feeling her nipples harden and strain toward his slowly descending mouth. The tip of his tongue circled, tantalized, and tested her desire before he enclosed the taut arousal with his lips. A glorious sense of anticipation rippled through her and she surrendered to the spiraling tension that promised such sweet fulfillment.

For a long while she lay passively beneath the light, erotic movements of his mouth, willing her pulse to slow its wild rush, and let Dain set the pace. She wanted to experience every touch, every sensation, to the fullest and then to give it all totally, lovingly, back to him.

Dain . . . Dain . . . Her heart murmured his name until it seemed to meld with each life-giving beat. Like the panorama of changing seasons, she visualized Dain loving her under the simmering blue sky of summer, on a pallet of autumn leaves, beside a red-gold fire on a snowy night and, again, as now, beneath a canopy of spring.

But as his hand made a smooth glide over the hollows and curves at her side, the fantasy faded into the breath-stealing reality of his touch. Her senses focused on the stimulating strokes of his fingertips as he pushed aside her jeans and the lacy underwear beneath to pave an unencumbered path for his lips to follow.

The path he chose began at the corner of her mouth, feathered along her cheek, and nibbled at the fleshy lobe of her ear. His tongue explored the smoothness of her neck and the indentations of her shoulders. Then he paused to admire what his lips had conquered.

Amanda quivered beneath that possessive gaze, but she remained still, savoring the look in his eyes and the quiet knowledge that he found her beautiful. When his hands brushed across her breasts and moved deliciously lower, she longed to hurry the lingering seduction. She wanted to taste his lips, to feel his fevered body pressing into hers, to know the urgency that precluded passion.

But she was powerless to hurry Dain. She was his captive, an impatient yet willing hostage of his caress. She drifted ever closer into his embrace like a leaf carried by a mountain stream.

His head bent to renew the sensation of a thousand sipping kisses against her skin. He explored the shadowy cleft between her breasts and his lips moved leisurely over the smooth swelling until, at last, he took the throbbing peak in his mouth.

The rough velvet of his palm against her inner thigh robbed her of reason and sent her hands in a blind search for the satisfaction she knew lay somewhere in the sinewy strength of his body. Mindlessly she rubbed the corded muscles of his neck and massaged the back of his shoulders. But Dain seemed determined to awaken every part of her with his kiss and he moved from her breast to the satiny flatness of her stomach.

His head lowered deliberately, creating an agony of anticipation inside her. With each downward foray of his tongue, her hands lost contact and she was soon unable to do more than fondle the hair at his temples.

His fingers parted and probed the intimate mysteries of her body and his lips branded every secret place with his burning possession. A wanton ache tightened her stomach and unfolded within her, building to a febrile heat that made her oddly pliant and yielding. She couldn't seem to breathe, but in this new world of sensation, breathing seemed too ordinary, too mundane to be a part of her. Dain's touch was the only reality, the only sustenance she needed.

"Dain." His name flowed from her on a sigh of surrender. Like a sacred promise it surrounded her in beauty, an offering of her heart that far transcended these few stolen moments in time.

"Dain." Again it echoed in the gentle silence, calling to him, asking him to claim the promise and return it to her lips.

The warm moistness of his mouth moved upward in response, lingering against her skin to feed the fire of her passion, clinging to the silken curves of her flesh to ignite the remaining embers of desire into flame.

She quivered with longing and her hands slid over him in stormy need, seeking to arouse in him the same fierce turbulence. Unbuttoning and parting the material of his shirt, her fingers tingled with the crisp feel of his chest. Her lips found the brown hardness of his nipple and plied it gently with her tongue as her hands stole around his waist to pull him tightly against her.

Dain moved free of her, despite her low moan of protest. She lifted desire-darkened eyes to watch as he shrugged off the shirt and unfastened the stud of his jeans. His clothes soon joined hers in a discarded heap and Amanda reveled in the sight of his tanned, virile body. Slowly, carefully, he covered her. His lips nuzzled her breast and ascended to the pulsing hollow of her throat. Then, at last, there was only the smooth tactile sensation of flesh against flesh, male against female.

Like a warm, tropical wind, ecstasy swirled inside her and rushed to meet his growing urgency. Amanda moved her hand to wedge a space between them, caressing him and guiding him toward the intimate union she craved. He cupped her hips, lifting her to accept the completeness of their coupling and the rhythmic dance of passion.

"Amanda . . ."

Her name blended with his as his breath filled her. She sank deeper into the delights of loving him, the taste and scent and feel of him merging with the music of her name on his lips. *Amanda . . . Amanda . . .*

"Amanda."

She snapped to the present with jarring speed and realized that Dain stood only a few feet away, repeating her name impatiently.

"I thought you were going to stay in the car." The abrasive quality of his voice tilted her chin in defense.

"I wanted to see for myself—" Her words ended in a painful, barely audible gasp as she looked past him to the clearing beyond. "Ohhh . . ." A wealth of sadness accompanied the sound and she took a step forward to see more clearly the upheaval that time had wrought. One of the sycamore trees had fallen. It lay sprawled across the clearing with roots exposed and lifeless branches disfiguring the brook's natural flow.

"Ohhh," she repeated quietly and turned to Dain.

A muscle worked in his cheek before he clamped it tight with a frown. "You should have stayed in the car. I would have told you."

But somehow Amanda knew that he wouldn't have. "What do you suppose could have happened?" she asked.

He thrust his hands into the back pockets of his jeans and surveyed the scene with dispassionate eyes. "Probably a combination of things. Shallow roots, a strong wind. I don't know. What does it matter?"

Her gaze swept the length of the tree and found the grassy bed where once she had lain in his embrace. Shadowed now by part of the fallen tree, it no longer reminded her of what had once been and, impulsively, her heart sought a way to deny the change.

"Maybe the ogre of the woods—?" A derisive silence followed her pitiful attempt to recapture the past and she wondered why she had even felt the urge to try.

Dain shrugged—a simple, eloquent shrug. "Well, whatever happened here, it seems like a fitting end. Come on, let's go. Martha is expecting us."

He pivoted and walked back to the path, leaving her to follow. Amanda hesitated as tears welled behind her eyes. She wasn't sure if she wanted to cry for the whim of nature that had spoiled this spot or if it was simply a need to shed a teardrop for the innocent girl who had once loved and been loved here.

A fitting end, she thought.

Blinking aside the emotion, Amanda turned and followed the path back to the car.

CHAPTER THREE

"More cider, Amanda?" Martha extended the silver coffee urn with a hopeful flourish and a doubtful smile.

With a shake of her head Amanda refused the third offer to replenish her cup. She took one last sip of the pungent drink and wished that Martha allowed something stronger than apple cider to be served in her home.

"What about you, Dain?" Martha swung in his direction to urge a refill. He sat in an overstuffed wing-back chair, looking very much at home with his feet propped on a matching hassock and dubiously eyeing the cup perched on the arm of his chair.

"What?" he asked absently, glancing first at Amanda and then at Martha. "Oh, no. No more cider. I've had all I can—all I need, thanks."

"I can't give the stuff away this year," Martha grumbled as she plopped the antique server onto the matching silver tray and arranged the rest of the tea service around it.

Amanda reprimanded her impulse to smile. Only Martha would serve cider in an heirloom tea service. Perhaps that was one of the reasons she seemed ageless. Martha never hesitated to do the things that gave her pleasure, no matter what anyone else might think. She was a mixture of youth and wisdom, her appearance a salt and pepper blend, her good nature spicy with humor and tart advice.

"Well, well, well." Martha folded her stout frame into a Boston rocker and surveyed Amanda with interest. The green eyes held a hint of their usual Irish blarney as they made a quick perusal. A visual inspection that Amanda ordinarily accepted as a matter of course.

But today, knowing that the affectionate light in Martha's eyes would soon dim in disappointment, Amanda was ill at ease. To conceal her discomfort she leaned forward to set her cup on the coffee table, then settled against the sofa cushions to await Martha's judgment.

"You're too thin, Amanda." The blunt criticism was softened with a wink as Martha turned to Dain. "You should take better care of her. She's wasting away to nothing."

Dain looked up, his gaze brushing Amanda in unconcern. "She's a long way from that, Martha. Amanda just needs a jug of your cider and some tender loving care."

Meeting his eyes with a lift of her brow, Amanda wondered at the teasing quality of his voice that wasn't really like teasing at all. "I draw the line at a 'jug' of cider," she said, trying to imitate his tone. "If I can't sip it from an eighteenth-century silver teacup then I'd rather do without."

"You can borrow mine anytime, Amanda," Martha said, "but you've got it wrong. You're supposed to sip cider from a sieve."

45

Amanda released a soft laugh from her tight throat. "That can't be right, Martha."

"You're both wrong." Dain straightened in his chair as if he were going to impart a priceless gem of wisdom. "I believe the correct adage is 'sipping champagne from a slipper,' which is an old tradition for bridegrooms on their wedding day."

"Humph!" Martha indicated her opinion. "I can't believe that any man would be so besotted he'd drink champagne or anything else from a shoe. You didn't do anything so silly on your wedding day, did you, Dain?"

His brown eyes met her blue ones in silent reminiscence and Amanda felt her lips tremble with the longing to smile.

"No, Martha," he said without breaking the moment of shared memory. "I certainly never drank champagne from Amanda's slipper."

Only because he'd spilled it halfway to his lips, Amanda remembered. And, unbidden, she remembered, too, the carefree way she'd giggled . . . until he had stilled her laughter with sipping kisses and the softly suggestive observation that no amount of champagne could compete with the intoxication of loving her.

Slowly, almost painfully, her lips curved upward to match his seemingly effortless smile.

"Well, I'm glad to see you two smiling for a change. You've both been so solemn this afternoon that I was beginning to think I'd have to give you a good talking to."

At Martha's words Amanda jerked free of Dain's gaze and tried, unsuccessfully, to keep the tiny smile from fading too fast. Somewhere in her heart she heard and echoed Dain's deep sigh.

He stood and paced to the wall of bookshelves. Although she wasn't watching, Amanda knew the precise moment he shoved his hands into his trouser pockets and turned to face Martha. "It's too late for lectures. Amanda and I are getting a divorce."

It was a cold, hard fact delivered in an impersonal tone that robbed the words of importance and left no room for argument. Exactly the way she had expected him to say it. Amanda stared down at her trembling hands. Exactly the way she'd secretly hoped he wouldn't be able to say it. Reluctantly, she lifted her gaze to Martha.

The vivacious, laughter-wrinkled face grew old as Martha struggled with Dain's simple announcement. "Oh, no, Dain," she said in a voice that grated with emotion. "I don't believe it. That couldn't happen to you and Amanda."

"It has already happened." Dain walked to the rocker where Martha sat and placed his hand on her shoulder. "I don't know why you're surprised. You've been telling me for years that she'd get enough of my foolishness and leave me one of these days."

With a frown Martha turned to glare up at him, obviously as taken aback by his flippant words as was Amanda. "I never believed she'd do it though," Martha snapped. "What's wrong with you, Dain? This is not something you joke about."

He withdrew his hand from her shoulder. "It isn't? All right, I'm open to suggestions. What is the 'proper' way to discuss the subject?"

Anger seeped through Amanda and she wanted to berate his callous attitude. But she couldn't be sure her voice wouldn't convey a world of regrets rather than the composure she wanted. Much better to avoid talking to him at all. "Martha?" she queried softly and waited for the green

47

eyes to focus on her. "I know what a shock this is for you and I'm sorry there wasn't a way to make it eas—"

"Sorry!" Martha scoffed. She stood, placing her hands on her hips and turning an admonishing stare to Dain. "And I suppose you're sorry too! Well, don't think you have any reason to apologize to me. Either one of you! I never thought you could do something so foolish, Dain." The stare swung to Amanda. "Or you either, for that matter."

Amanda felt suddenly awkward and guilty, as if she'd left twenty of her twenty-eight years on the doorstep. She sought for something to bridge the gap and return her to equal footing with the older woman. "Martha, it's just one of those things that—"

"Fools!" Martha interrupted gruffly. "Damn fools! Both of you."

"Martha, leave her alone." Dain's command altered the tension immediately and bridged the gap for Amanda. "The decision is made. Amanda could use your support, not this pointless castigation. As I said, she needs your tender loving care now."

"And what about your promise to give her tender loving care, Dain? A promise that was supposed to last a lifetime. What about that?"

"Nothing lasts forever," he answered with a shrug. "Circumstances change. People change. Some promises aren't made to be kept."

Amanda tried not to show any surprise at his casual answer, but she couldn't curb the hurt that wove through her. She felt Martha's sharp look and forced herself to meet it. Searchingly, with slicing perception, the gaze examined Amanda before sliding back to Dain with angry challenge.

"That's a namby-pamby excuse," Martha said tightly. "You've hardly been married long enough to know the meaning of a lasting promise . . . and to quit! Give up without a fight! I expected better from you, Dain. And you, Amanda. How can you even consider—"

"We're not considering a divorce, Martha," Dain interrupted her tirade with firm insistence. "The decision is made. Nothing you say can change that. Accept our decision and give Amanda the support she needs."

Amanda's feeling of hurt gave way to irritation that Dain again referred to her need for support and pointedly ignored his own—if he felt the need for support at all. "He's right, Martha." Amanda added impact to Dain's statements with a smooth voice and a deliberate tilt of her chin. "The decision is made—irrevocably."

"And the sooner we all accept it, the better." Martha sank back onto the Boston rocker, her words, her eyes, even her posture admitting constrained resignation. "Is that the proper attitude?" Her gaze sought Dain in one last appeal for denial.

Amanda wanted to look away from this obvious hurt, so unintentionally inflicted. She wanted to look away and yet she found her own gaze seeking Dain, seeking acceptance or denial or perhaps merely a hint of regret.

The muscle in his jaw clenched and relaxed, clenched and relaxed, the only sign of his tension, or was it just impatience? "Yes, that's it," he said finally, blandly, indifferently. "The sooner the better."

Of its own accord, Amanda's gaze fell. Impatience. She recognized the sound of it. Dain wanted this uncomfortable discussion at an end. He wanted his marriage over. And he wanted her out of his life. The sooner the better.

And that was what she wanted too. With a resolute sigh

she leaned against the tapestried sofa cushions and waited for Martha to assimilate the inevitable and break the cloistered silence.

Silence. Dain hated it. Almost as much as he hated the stricken look in Martha's eyes. Almost as much as he hated the schooled composure of Amanda's expression. He forced himself to stand, relaxed and waiting, although he was tense with the need to pace the room. His eyes traced the familiar, book-lined wall, the uneven combination of antique and merely dated furnishings, the woven rug covering the floor. Anywhere except at the slender figure of Amanda.

Yet he knew, without seeing, the quiet clasp of hands in her lap, the concern mirrored in the twilight softness of her eyes as she watched Martha, the regrets, the memories, that calm, impenetrable façade.

Would he ever be free of knowing her? Even now her very stillness spoke to him in the silence. But he couldn't trust himself to interpret the meaning anymore. She had changed and he couldn't begin to guess at her thoughts. He might misunderstand, say the wrong thing and send her further away from him.

Dain carefully shielded the gaze that, despite his control, slid to her. There wasn't anything he could say that would send Amanda further away. She was as distant to him as the sun's fire and yet still as near as its warming rays. Pressing his lips tight in determination, Dain turned away. If only he could make it through this confrontation with Martha. Avoid her prying, too perceptive eyes and not lose his hardwon control, maybe, just maybe . . .

"All right," Martha shattered the quiet. "Tell me why. I want to know what happened."

Sensing Amanda's immediate tension, Dain pinned

50

Martha with a falsely amused gaze. "She never puts the cap back on the toothpaste. I leave wet towels in the shower. That's it!"

"Dain!" Amanda straightened as his name rolled from her lips on a breath of annoyance. How could he speak so . . . so superficially of their marriage? "Don't say such—" Her voice broke and she felt the threat of tears at the base of her throat. With a jerky motion she turned toward Martha. "He doesn't mean to sound . . ."

"How do you know how I meant to sound, Amanda? Or what I really meant to say?"

"I know you're being facetious, Dain. You don't see the break-up of our marriage as a result of wet towels and toothpaste. I know you don't and so does Martha, so stop trying to make this a humorous discussion."

He swept her a mocking bow. "I would never do anything so crass, but I have no intention of discussing the gory details with Martha."

Amanda stared at him as his eyes darkened with a hint of frost. For probably the hundredth time in the past few days she wished she knew how to talk to him again.

"Perhaps you need to discuss the details with Amanda." Martha crossed her arms over her ample bosom and settled back in the rocking chair. "Maybe you both need to talk this thing out."

The militant gleam in Martha's eyes was unmistakable, and Amanda knew she and Dain were being maneuvered into a revealing discussion. It was time to put an end to the well-meaning but misguided interference. "The time for talking is past," she said quietly. "Sometimes it's important to know when to quit trying, Martha. I hope you'll understand, but, either way, it doesn't change anything.

As soon as I find a place to live, my marriage to Dain is over."

The awesome finality of what she was doing washed over her and Amanda wondered that she could remain so detached. Almost as if she were an observer and not a participant in the conversation. From force of habit her gaze swiveled in Dain's direction to share this odd sensation. But she discovered only the broad expanse of his back and the strong fingers that wearily massaged his nape. She would have to remind him to get a haircut, she thought, and then closed her eyes at the inanity of it.

"You could stay here with me." Martha's voice came, strained but accepting. "There's plenty of room and—"

"Thank you." Amanda shook her head and offered a thread of a smile. "But I think I should be on my own. I—I just need to be alone."

"You could use the cottage," Martha urged. "It's been vacant for a couple of months and I've been meaning to call the agent about listing it as a rental again. It needs some attention, but I would love to have you close by, Amanda." Martha pursed her lips in a self-contained appeal. "I won't interfere. And if I forget, you can tell me to mind my own damn business."

Amanda refrained from mentioning that telling Martha to mind her own business and having her do so were not one and the same. Still, thoughts of the cottage were tempting. It was on the far corner of Martha's land, nestled inconspicuously along an inlet of Chesapeake Bay. A place of quietly lapping water and tall evergreens. A good place for thinking . . . for healing.

"I'd like to rent the house, Martha, but only on condition that I pay the same rent as anyone else. No favors, all right?"

"Humph! Favors?" Martha said with a quicksilver flash of humor. "I don't believe in that sort of thing. You'll pay the same—no, I take that back. You'll pay more. That seems only fair. Don't you think so, Dain?"

He stood staring out the window, as if he hadn't heard . . . or didn't care.

"Dain?" Martha repeated her attempt to gain his attention.

Slowly he turned, his expression a study of indifference. "I'm sure you'll be fair with Amanda. And I'm equally sure she'll be happy, wonderfully happy, living in the cottage. Alone."

Drawn by the intensity in his voice, Amanda searched his face for a clue to his feelings. He was behaving so strangely today. With a sigh, she lowered her gaze. What did she expect? Of course he wasn't himself. This was as awkward and uncomfortable for him as for her. The tension in the room was so heavy, it could have been bottled and sold by weight.

Happy. Alone. His words lay somberly in her mind. It had been some time since she'd experienced either state. But she needed to be alone and she would learn to be happy again. Maybe not right away, not tomorrow. But soon. Soon.

At the end of the month Amanda moved into her new home. Martha's cottage was a two-story frame house with a back deck that faced the bay. Dain pronounced the exterior structurally sound and left the condition of the interior to Amanda. Surprisingly she didn't find the torn wallpaper and pallid walls dismaying but saw, instead, a challenge. Her training in interior design and her innate sense of color kept creating visions of redecorated rooms complete with new draperies and furnishings.

With each box she carried into the house, Amanda found herself stopping to weigh the merits of one color against another or the effect a particular fabric might produce. More than once Dain had to prod her from the imaginary redecorating to the more pressing activity of moving in.

He had been insistent upon helping her "get settled" and Amanda hadn't been able to fault his cautious friendliness, although she'd tried. He was making the move easy, taking care of details that might trouble her. And, perversely, she wanted him to be less helpful, less concerned. His careful attitude told her that he still felt a certain amount of responsibility for her well-being. At times Amanda wished he would dispense with the pretense, and at other times she wished his outward concern was real.

But she knew that all pretense between them would soon be at an end. She had already made the appointment to see an attorney next week. When she'd told Dain, he'd simply nodded, seemingly anxious to get her settled and begin anew—without her. It was understandable, of course. She felt the same way, didn't she? And she thought it was probably perfectly natural to feel a sadness, a sense of disappointment at this time.

Tactfully, Dain had left her to pack whatever she wanted to take from their home. He offered no suggestions and no protests when he saw the two small boxes that hid her most treasured mementos. She was glad he couldn't see inside the boxes to the sentiment they sheltered.

Somehow she didn't want him to know what she had chosen to keep. The scrapbook of pictures, the rose now dried and faded but still scented with remembrance, a charm bracelet, a book of poetry, a conch shell endlessly whispering of happier days, the pudgy stuffed bear Dain had given her when she was so discouraged about ever conceiving a child, the tiny shoes meant for her son, but never worn. So many little things that reminded her, would always remind her. She wanted nothing else.

Still there were things that couldn't be left behind and, reluctantly, Amanda packed these too. She took only what she would need for the cottage and left decisions about the rest to Dain's discretion.

Moving day brought a sense of purpose and a lightening of her mood. Dain seemed decidedly cheerful as he carried clothing and boxes from the house to the car and then later, from the car into the cottage. He talked casually about the weather, the nice view from the deck, how he planned to get in some sailing soon. Everyday type of conversation, easy and amicable, as if there were nothing unusual about the day.

"Beautiful day for this," Dain said as he walked through the front doorway and stepped around Amanda and over the clutter in the hall to reach the stairs. The box he held firmly against his chest muffled the rest of his words, but Amanda caught the gist of them before he disappeared into the upstairs bedroom. "Beautiful day for transporting boxes," he mumbled. "Or swimming. Or playing tennis. Or sailing. Beautiful day for sailing."

Amanda recognized his good-natured grumbling and ignored it as she always did, or always used to do. The qualification made a small rent in the day's equanimity, but she forced herself to ignore that as well. Digging deeper into the disorganized box before her, she released a satisfied sigh as her fingers closed around the sack of nails she sought. With a flashlight nestled in the crook of her arm, she grasped the hammer in one hand, the nails in the other, and levered to her feet.

Approaching the closet beneath the stairs, she carefully propped the door open and squinted into the dusty interior. A row of wooden shelves slanted along the wall in a useless forty-five-degree angle. But not for long, Amanda thought as she pushed the stepladder inside. She took a few nails from the sack and transferred them to her mouth before mounting the three-tiered ladder with hammer, flashlight, and determination.

Juggling the shelves into place proved somewhat more difficult than she had envisioned and securing them to the wall proved impossible. When she heard Dain's footsteps on the stairs, she opened her mouth to call him, dropped the nails, followed swiftly by the flashlight and a muttered "Damn!"

The closet became even darker as Dain leaned against the doorframe and blocked the outside light. "Ah, just as I suspected," he observed dryly. "A goblin under the stairs."

Amanda frowned down at him. "Funny. Would you mind holding the shelves at the bottom so I can nail them in place?"

"And have you drop the hammer on my foot?" Dain shook his head and stepped inside the closet. "No, thanks. I can be of more assistance up there with you, not to mention being safe from falling objects."

"Dain, there isn't room." She finished the protest even as he made room in the narrow space. With his feet on the rung below her, his thighs cushioned the curve of her hips. His arms slipped around her on either side and he pushed the shelves into the correct position.

For a suspended moment Amanda was breathless at the

warm sensations coursing through her. It had been such a long time since he'd been this close, since her body had conformed so perfectly to his. She felt the familiar responses stir inside her and wished, for that single moment, that she could relax against him and lose herself in his strength.

His lips were only inches from her temple and his voice was a delicious ruffling of her ebony curls. "See? There's plenty of room, Amanda. Besides, we've been in closer quarters than this, haven't we?"

It was a needless reminder. She fairly ached with the memory. But this was the wrong place, the wrong time for remembering. "Hold that still," she said roughly, and concentrated her energies on the closet shelf.

"Are you sure you can see to do this?" he asked. "Do you want me to—"

"Just hold it and keep your thumb out of the way."

"If you hit my thumb, we're both in big trouble. Are you positive you can see what you're—"

The hammer struck the nail squarely, but the motion propelled her back against his muscular chest. His arms tightened around her to restore balance, yet her senses reeled with his nearness and she felt totally off balance. Had she forgotten how gentle his touch could be? How scintillating his maleness felt next to her?

For a fleeting moment Amanda let her body reminisce. The embers of forgotten fires smoldered within her and her lips parted on a low sigh of memory. She knew the instant he became aware of her stillness and she felt the tension ripple through him as she lingered in his arms for a second too long.

"Maybe I should let you do this, Dain." She ended the careful embrace and waited for him to step from the ladder before she followed. Free of the intimate darkness in the closet, she drew her composure safely into place. "Do you want me to help?" she asked as an afterthought when he took the hammer from her hand and remounted the steps.

"No. I can manage."

His voice sounded natural with no hint of strain, but Amanda knew there would be little, if any further conversation between them. The lighthearted mood had been shattered by that second of awareness, by the knowledge that what they had once shared could not be recaptured and yet could never truly be lost to them either.

It was time for good-bye, but Amanda made coffee and Dain obligingly drank a cup. When he placed the mug in the sink and turned to her with a resolute arch of his brow, she nodded and walked with him to the door. Dain stopped to check the security lock one last time before he stepped outside.

Thrusting her hands into the back pockets of her jeans, Amanda followed him onto the front porch. Sunlight still rimmed the surrounding trees, but the scent of evening was already in the air. It would be cool here at night, she thought absently. She would need a blanket to keep warm.

Her gaze followed the sun's rays to Dain. He stood with his hand resting on the wooden support, the breeze from the bay teasing a strand of his tawny hair. The image burrowed deep inside her, despite her wish not to remember. She felt vulnerable and hoped for a quick, painless good-bye.

As he turned toward her she turned away. "Since you're moved out, and in, I guess I'll be on my way." His voice seemed to cross a great distance before it finally reached her.

"Yes." She couldn't look at him. She wanted to, but she couldn't. She should say something, but she couldn't think what it should be. "Thank you," she managed at last.

"You're welcome . . . Amanda." He said her name in such a husky whisper that she had no alternative but to face him. Their eyes met and held to exchange a silent reluctance at this last parting.

Her lips quivered with indecision and finally found a smile. "Do we shake hands now?"

He exhaled a breath, too deep to be natural, too soft for a sigh. "No, Amanda. Not this time."

Her heart stopped beating as he moved to cup her fingers in his palm. Slowly his thumb began to stroke the back of her hand and raw emotion built in her throat. He was going to kiss her one more time. A farewell kiss. Dear heaven, how would she get through it?

Irrelevantly, her thoughts wandered. Obscure scenes drifted to the surface of her mind—Romeo and Juliet sharing dawn's final kiss, Scarlett O'Hara watching Rhett Butler walk into the gray Atlanta mist, Bogart and Bergman in the fading scene of *Casablanca*. And now, Dain drawing her slowly, inexorably, into his arms for this . . . their last good-bye.

Staring helplessly into his umber eyes, she remembered the first time he'd kissed her. The sweet sense of anticipation that had preceded the first taste of his lips. She had known then, as she knew now, that Dain would take more than a kiss. Then he had taken her heart. Now he would take the threads of the past and tie them in a tidy knot for her.

As he lowered his head she closed her eyes and prayed that she could hold on to her self-control.

Dain paused just a breath from Amanda's lips. He was

uncertain now as he had never been before. Why had he decided to kiss her? It would only prolong this already bittersweet good-bye. Did he hope for a response? A sign? A hint that she wanted him to stay? It wouldn't happen. She was tense in his arms and although he could see the betraying trembling of her lips, he knew it was not the betrayal of emotion that he wanted to see.

He caressed the outline of her mouth with his gaze, wishing he could do so with a fingertip. The first time he'd kissed her he had touched her lips hesitantly, wondrously aware of her fragile beauty. Was it possible that she had grown more lovely since then or did he see her now with an experienced eye, attuned to her beauty within?

Slowly he defied the space that separated their lips, even as his heart defied the distance she had placed between them. You're mine, Amanda, he told her silently. This is just a new beginning for us. I can't, I won't say good-bye.

The warmth of his touch kindled inside her, but Amanda refused to fan the flame. She didn't want this kiss and yet her arms moved to hold him close, even though she knew their closeness was only an illusion, existing physically but in no other way.

Her lips responded to his as they always had. She had no control over them, just as she seemed to have little control over the wild throbbing of her pulse and the trembling of her legs. And she had no defense against his tenderness.

The necessity of their parting lost meaning for her as the kiss deepened and then softened with lingering sweetness. It was almost over and Amanda didn't know how she could let him go. She felt a sharp stab of regret and the anguish of a thousand reasons searching for a single rhyme.

Then Dain was pulling away, his eyes liquid dark. He brought his palm up to warm her cheek for the brief span of a heartbeat. "Something to remember me by," he whispered.

Pressing her lips tightly together, Amanda lifted her chin, straightened her shoulders, and turned to enter the house. She heard his departing footsteps, listened to the sounds of his leaving. Then she closed the door.

Without actually intending to, she began unpacking and putting things away. She paid no heed to the salty teardrops that trickled one after another down her cheek.

Something to remember me by.

As if she could forget.

CHAPTER FOUR

Gray blended into cream, softened to gold, and fused with palest pink in a gentle harmony. It was a subtle room. A room for quiet music, a good book, or deep thoughts. There wasn't a piece of furniture or a picture on the wall that didn't reflect the awakening shades of dawn. From floor to ceiling and back again the colors flowed in one smooth statement of taste.

Amanda stood in the doorway and remembered how the room had looked on the day she'd moved in. It had been worn and tired, giving no invitation to rest or relax within its perimeters. It hadn't suited her then. But now that the redecorating was complete, she wasn't sure it suited her any better.

It was lovely, gleaming, inviting, and she had thoroughly enjoyed choosing fabric, accessories, and new furniture. The entire house had been a challenge that she had welcomed and tackled with fervor. From a new coat of paint on the back deck to the no-wax shine on the kitchen floor to the crisp Priscilla curtains on the bedroom window, the shabby house had been redone.

Martha dubbed the renovation a "blooming miracle." Expensive, but a miracle just the same. It would have been nicer, of course, if a touch of kelly green had been splashed here and there. But Martha was quick to add that she wasn't a decorator and that she didn't have to live with the shrinking-violet colors. Accepting the comments in the constructively critical manner in which they were meant, Amanda had merely smiled at Martha's many "suggestions."

In truth, Amanda had surprised herself a little in redecorating the house. Ordinarily she preferred at least a few vivid sparks of color in a room. She hadn't consciously omitted a touch of brightness this time; it just hadn't happened.

Funny, she thought now as she slipped off her shoes and walked into the living room. The quiet whisper of her nylons against the carpet sifted richly through the air. Her fingers glided over the polished cotton material of the sofa and draperies. She inhaled the fragrance of fresh paint and new things. Everything pleased her and yet it didn't seem quite right; it didn't feel like home.

Reluctantly, she let her thoughts drift home. They hadn't far to go. The house she and Dain had planned and built came to mind each time she entered this room. Perhaps it was because the contrast between that house and this one was so patently obvious. As obvious as the contrast within herself, Amanda decided. Then she had been a vibrant, alive splash of color; now she was a blend of the subdued tones surrounding her.

And it was a softening that Amanda thought she would like once she became accustomed to it. There was so much

63

to discover about this new Amanda that had evolved slowly from the old. She was awakening to a different awareness of life, just as this old room had taken on the gentle promise of a new morning.

Amanda sat on the edge of the sofa and stretched lazily. Tomorrow she was going to awaken to the demands of a new job. She could still hardly believe that she'd finally resigned her position as design consultant at an exclusive Baltimore department store. It was a job that had lost its appeal over the past few years and had given her an outlet during the confusing months after the baby's death. It had taken only a week after she'd moved into this house for her to resign, clean out her desk, and leave the store without a backward glance or a trace of regret. She was ready for a change in her life so she hadn't missed it. It was simply an example of something that had once been important and now no longer mattered. She was finding a lot of those "somethings" in her everyday routine. And, oddly, she was discovering it was the little, unimportant things that she missed. Things like sharing a comfortable silence over a cup of coffee or knowing, in the drowsy moments just before sleep, that there was a familiar someone nearby. It had been a long time since she'd shared those things. Since long before she'd moved here. So why did she miss them now?

Amanda sighed and pushed to her feet. She missed them now because they were beyond her reach. The stiff white papers in her desk drawer were a potent reminder that, barring complications, she would be officially single in a matter of months. Her signature on those papers was all that was required before the petition for divorce could be filed. Amanda Stuart Maxwell versus Dain Cameron Maxwell.

Closing her eyes, she rubbed her forehead, but the words still blazed starkly eloquent in her mind. Amanda versus Dain. How concise. How simplistic. How piercingly ironic. She wondered how Dain would feel when he received his copy of the papers, and then blocked the thoughts from her consciousness.

She would be late for dinner at Martha's if she didn't get moving. It was the first dinner invitation she'd accepted and she didn't want to risk a good-natured scolding when she did arrive. With a quick, reassuring scan of her green button-front skirt and white blouse, she left the house to walk the half-mile or so that separated her from Martha's.

Summer bloomed, hot and humid, along the path and Amanda filled her lungs with the stuffy heat. By the time she reached the carved, double doors of the house and lifted the ornate knocker, the heat had entered her cheeks and spiraled damply into the limp curls at her nape.

"Come in, come in." Martha motioned Amanda into the air-conditioned hall and surveyed her with disapproval. "You look like you could be second cousin to a heat stroke. Go on in the front room and make yourself comfortable. I'll get you something to drink."

"Hello, Martha." Amanda pointedly addressed the sturdy back bustling away in the direction of the kitchen, but Martha paid no heed. With a wry lift of her brow, Amanda did as she was bid and relaxed in the comforting coolness.

"Whatever possessed you to walk in the first place?" Martha entered the room at the same brisk pace and presented Amanda with a modified version of a mint julep.

Accepting the sun-brewed tea laced with cider and a sprig of mint, Amanda smiled a thank-you. She accepted the fussing in the same spirit, knowing that if she had chosen to drive, Martha would have scolded her for not getting enough exercise. Martha was a mother hen in search of a chick, and at the moment Amanda happened to be the chick closest at hand.

"Feel better?" Martha asked as she eased herself onto the edge of the Boston rocker.

"I feel fine," Amanda stated firmly. "I felt fine when I arrived on your doorstep. It's only a short walk, Martha, and it's only a little humid outside. You worry too much."

Her wrinkled cheeks creased with a smile. "I worry about you cooped up in that house with wallpaper samples and fabric scraps. You need to get out, Amanda. Meet people. Find out what's going on in the world."

Amanda swirled the glass in her hand until ice cubes clinked musically. She could feel a lecture hiding behind that bland smile; Martha was ever on the alert for her opportunity. "I do get out, Martha. I'm here. And I spent the entire day in Annapolis—meeting people. In fact I have a job beginning first thing in the morning."

"A job? You mean you're going to work?"

"I'm afraid so," Amanda said with a teasing laugh. "No more goofing off for me and no more free interior decorating for you. Tomorrow I join the eight-to-five rank and file. Well, actually, it will be nine to three. I'll be working for Susan Williams at her child-care center. Imagine me with a group of rowdy preschoolers! Lucky I took some college hours in early childhood education, wasn't it?" Amanda stopped to sip at her drink, hoping Martha wouldn't notice the breathy uncertainty in her voice, but knowing she couldn't help but notice.

"Children?" The word came cautiously, accompanied

66

by a watchful green gaze. "Is that the sort of work you want to do, Amanda?"

Straightforward, Amanda thought. No "Do you think that's wise?" or "Can you handle it?" or "How can you be around children every day and not be constantly remembering and regretting?" None of the questions she had asked herself again and again. Just a concerned look and a straightforward question. That was Martha's way and Amanda knew she wouldn't get by with a yes or no answer.

"I think it is," Amanda said. "At first I wasn't sure, but after I visited the center and looked around, I decided to give it a try." She paused to glance away from the perceptive gaze. "I love children, Martha, and I can't spend my entire life avoiding them just because I might feel uncomfortable at times."

She didn't attempt any further explanation. How could she explain? How could she tell anyone else the curious pleasure she had felt when she walked into the center today? No one else would understand her motives; her longing to love and enjoy the delights of children without risking her still tender emotions. Perhaps it was selfish, but surely no one could be hurt if she shared a moment of childish wonder or stole an innocent smile. . . .

"What?" Amanda snapped to attention at the mention of the name.

Martha assumed a knowing frown. "I said what is Dain going to think?"

The odd tightening of her throat returned unexpectedly and Amanda swallowed hard to dislodge it. "I doubt that he'll be interested enough to think anything."

"Would you be interested if you heard that he'd sold out and was going to work for another architect?"

"What?" Amanda sat straighter in surprise. "Dain sold the firm? I can't believe it!"

Folding her arms, Martha smiled and began to rock. "I didn't say he sold the firm. I just asked if you'd be interested to know it if he did."

Amanda sighed her impatience and tried not to admit it was also a sigh of relief. "You never give up, do you?"

"You didn't answer me, Amanda."

Lifting her palms in defeat, she capitulated. "All right, Martha. Yes, I'd be interested. But, then, so would dozens of other people."

"You know what I meant."

In a fluid rhythm of composure, Amanda set her tea glass on the table, crossed one knee over the other, and clasped her hands in her lap. "Let's drop the subject."

"Let's not." Martha leaned forward, her eyes bright with eagerness to countermand the blasé tone of her voice. "You need to talk about Dain sometime. You can't go on jumping every time his name is mentioned."

"I don't—"

"You do."

Agitated, Amanda stood and then wasn't certain of what action to initiate next. It bothered her to know that Martha was right and it bothered her even more to realize that she was interested, insatiably so, in gleaning tidbits of information about Dain. On a breath of surrender Amanda sat back down. "How is he, Martha?"

"Working too hard," came the crisp, almost accusing, answer. "He calls most nights from the office. I suppose he's spending a lot of time there."

Amanda nodded. "The Reichmann account, I'll bet. I know he was completing the scale models for that hotel chain. Just think, one day we'll walk into a hotel in another country and recognize Dain as the architect. Won't that be marvelous?"

"For some of us."

"Martha, please. Just because Dain and I aren't—" She had to stop and swallow again—hard. "I'll always be very proud of him."

Martha gave an audible sniff. "You once said you'd always love him."

How could she answer that? "I know," she said quietly. "I know."

"Let's eat." Martha rolled to her feet and walked to the doorway with a cursory glance at Amanda. "We're having Chinese tonight. Stringy vegetables with globs of rice and Lord only knows what else. I made the mistake of letting Mr. MacGregor buy a wok, and he's starving me to death. . . ."

Amanda's gaze followed her hostess from the room, but her mind was a little slow to catch up. The change of topic had been deliberate, of course. Martha was never subtle, but she had a way of making her point. With a shake of her head Amanda rose and started toward the dining room. Dain was in her thoughts now, as he hadn't been before. His absence was an empty feeling that surrounded her and would almost certainly linger for the rest of the evening.

Martha. You couldn't trust her for a minute.

As Amanda entered the room and seated herself, Martha smiled complacently. She waited a moment before bracing her hands on either side of her plate and challenging the burly man standing beside her. "All right, Mr. MacGregor, bring it on."

"With chopsticks or without?" he asked with brusque amusement.

69

"Without, you sorry excuse for a cook!"

Not by the blink of an eye did he let Martha intimidate him as he turned to Amanda with a wide grin. "You'll like supper, Amanda. I know you appreciate fine cuisine."

Martha leaned close to rasp a whisper. "Don't you dare encourage him. He's unbearable as it is. I don't know why I keep him around."

That was something Amanda had often wondered herself. She lifted a finger to her lips to quell their tendency to smile and remembered the first time she'd met Mr. MacGregor. He had been there just one day, acting as chef, butler, gardener, and generally aggravating Martha. There had been no explanations, only a brief introduction, and after that he was simply a member of the household. Even now Amanda had no idea if he had a first name other than Mister.

She liked him, liked the crusty way he talked and the faded blue of his eyes. And she liked the way he handled Martha. Amanda's curiosity had pushed forth a dozen possible definitions of the relationship, but none of them seemed to fit. She remembered asking Dain what he thought.

"Well, if you want my opinion," he'd replied with a slyly suspicious arching of his brow. "I suspect that Martha and MacGregor are living in sin."

Amanda had gasped in shocked surprise. "Dain! You don't mean—"

"Yes." Dain had frowned in mocking sobriety. "I suspect they are carrying on right in this very house. And you know what else, Amanda?"

"What?" She had practically fallen off her chair waiting for Dain to continue.

"It's none of our business."

Of course, it hadn't been then and it wasn't now. There had never been an iota of evidence to support the idea. But there had been none to discredit the possibility either. And she did wonder. . . .

Amanda let her lips tip up at the corners and wished Dain were here to speculate with her again.

"See, Amanda? What did I tell you?" Martha gave a disparaging look at the food being placed on the table. "It's a miracle that I haven't gotten sick eating all this health food."

"You're never sick, Martha." Amanda thought the food looked appetizing and smelled even better. "It must be all those vitamins you take."

"Vitamins?" Martha grumbled as she ladled extremely healthy portions onto her own and Amanda's plates. "It's good, clean living. That's what it is."

Amanda couldn't resist the laughter that welled in her throat and her gaze automatically crossed the table to share.

Loneliness closed around her like a cold December day. Dain should be there and he wasn't. She should be looking into brown eyes spiced with laughter and she was staring at an empty chair. Oh, Dain. Her heart twisted with missing him.

Dinner passed in a superficial haze of conversation. Martha talked about something, but Amanda didn't really pay much attention. She supposed she made the proper responses, smiled at the right times, but her mind was caught in a tide of memories that ebbed and flowed through her consciousness. A reminder of Dain called to her from every corner of the room and superseded Martha's words to plunge deep into the past and reminisce.

Images bathed in the perspective of time; glimpses of

moments, indistinct in their importance except for the quiet pleasure they evoked. Dain, captured in a heartbeat, for her own private portfolio. How strange that she had fought these memories, chased them from her whenever they appeared. Yet now, unexpectedly, to the accompaniment of a mundane conversation, she welcomed that which she had forbidden herself to recall.

She felt warmed by her thoughts of Dain and curiously comforted by the admission that she missed him. Even when she followed Martha into the front room again and resumed her place on the sofa, Amanda let the memories drift at will. Was it a good sign? Was her heart finally accepting the past, both painful and sweet? Would there be times, like now, when she could wrap herself in memories and not be afraid?

She sipped at the coffee Martha had so thoughtfully provided and was grateful for the companionable silence. Perhaps she was entering a new phase of healing. Perhaps this was a natural progression of emotion. Perhaps one day she really would feel whole again.

"You're very quiet tonight." Martha set the rocker into a gentle, mesmerizing motion. "Would you like to tell me where your thoughts have been all evening?"

Amanda let her lips slant in a fleeting confession. "I'm sorry. I suppose I haven't been very good company, have I?"

"The nice thing about family is that you don't have to pretend. I may not be your blood kin, Amanda, but we're family just the same. The first time I saw Dain when he was just a tow-headed, obstinate little boy, I knew he belonged to me in a special way. And I knew when he brought you to meet me that you belonged too. Children of my heart, Amanda. That's how I feel about you and

Dain." Martha curved thick fingers around the arms of the rocker and pinched her mouth tightly over her emotions. "I hurt for you," she said after a moment. "For both of you."

The bittersweet reminiscing slipped from her grasp and Amanda faced numbing reality again. "I know, Martha. I just don't know what to say, except that I believe the hard part is over. From now on it's just a matter of adjustment."

"Adjustment." Martha repeated the word with a shake of her head. Her green eyes assessed Amanda and looked away as if to conceal her skepticism. "Do you still love him, Amanda?"

Amanda's hand jerked slightly and coffee sloshed to the edge of the cup and splashed onto her skirt. In a sort of panicky indecision she grabbed a napkin and dabbed at the stain, but her efforts were as futile as her wish to escape an answer to the question.

Slowly she laid the napkin aside and raised uncertain blue eyes to Martha. "I don't know how to answer that," she said. "How can I deny something that has been a part of me for so long? How can I say I don't love him anymore when something inside me aches with the very thought of him? We shared some exquisite moments, a thousand intimate details of life. We had a son." She closed her eyes against the memory and released her emotion on a sigh. "Yes, I still love Dain. But, Martha, I just don't have the *will* to love him anymore."

"Amanda, I . . ." The desire to understand glistened in her eyes as Martha searched for something to say. The shrill tone of the telephone jarred the silence once and then again before Martha rose to answer. With her hand on the receiver she turned to Amanda. "This will be Dain," she said evenly. "He calls every night to check—"

The phone rang again and Martha lifted it to her ear. "Hello? . . . Yes, Dain. . . . Yes, fine. . . . Have you eaten? . . . Well, you should be glad you weren't here to see what Mr. MacGregor tried to pass off as dinner. I could hardly swallow a bite. . . ."

Amanda concealed her acute interest in eavesdropping by turning her head and pretending to study a speck of dust on the coffee table. She knew her every movement was watched and evaluated by Martha, but it didn't really matter. The rapid flutter of her pulse and the stirring of excitement within her could be hidden from view, but Amanda knew and recognized their import.

Dain was near. She could feel his presence, knew the husky resonance of his voice was only an insignificant distance from her ear. In her imagination she crossed the room and took the phone from Martha's hand. *Dain? This is Amanda,* she would say as if he wouldn't know. *How are you? Are you at the office or at home—*

No, she shouldn't mention home. That was too intimate . . . too much "theirs."

Dain? I've redecorated the cottage. You should come to see . . .

But he wouldn't.

Do you go out much, Dain? Do you ever see any of our old friends?

No, she couldn't just casually toss that into the conversation.

Have you been sailing, Dain? It's beautiful weather for sailing, isn't it?

No, too impersonal.

Dain? You've been in my thoughts all evening. I miss you.

No. No, she couldn't say something so revealing . . . so personal . . . so inadequate.

Amanda licked dry lips at the realization that there was nothing to say after she said hello. More than anything, at the moment, she wanted to hear his voice. But then what? Awkward silence? Or, worse, a forced effort to keep the tone of the conversation friendly?

With grudging acceptance she picked up the threads of Martha's chatter, knowing that eavesdropping was as close as Dain would be to her tonight.

"You know better, Dain Cameron Maxwell." Martha punctuated the words with a scolding click of her tongue. "I do not exaggerate and I never lie. She's too thin and I know she's not sleeping well."

Amanda froze to attention as she realized they were talking about her. Tilting her chin at an indignant angle, she turned to give Martha a warning glare which was, of course, totally ineffective.

"It doesn't matter how I know," Martha stated crossly to the telephone receiver. "If you saw her, you'd see for yourself—" The pause stretched unbearably and Amanda alternated between feeling irritated at being the object of discussion and feeling oddly pleased that Dain would even ask about her. "Why don't you ask her?" Martha said. "She's right here."

Like the last leaf of autumn, Amanda hung suspended, waiting, hoping for the chance to hear his voice once more. She composed her eagerness into a questioning frown and looked helplessly at Martha.

Dain's answer appeared first as disappointment in Martha's green eyes and then as cool disapproval in her voice.

"You must do what you think best, I suppose. But you might at least listen to my advice once in a while. It couldn't do any harm to talk to her. All right, all right. I'll mind my own business, but you're making a big mistake."

Amanda's eagerness vanished beneath a wave of distressingly unsatisfying rationale. Dain didn't want to speak to her. He didn't need to hear her voice. He probably didn't miss her at all. And that was good, she told herself firmly. She didn't want him to feel responsible for her or to cling to the past. It was better not to talk with him, of course. He'd realized that right away, even if she hadn't. But she couldn't remain in the room while he and Martha sparred over her well-being.

Amanda rose and walked sedately toward the door, although she wanted to run from the room. She even managed a half-smile when Martha motioned for her to stop.

With a shake of her head Amanda mouthed a "see you later" and lifted her hand in good-bye. She heard Martha's gruff, "Now, Dain, see what you've done? She's left." Amanda pulled the front door closed behind her and stepped into the twilight.

It was soothing, this indigo evening. Quiet and restful and nice. She could bathe in its stillness, absorb the night sounds, and cover the noisy clutter inside her. By the time she reached home she could be as calm and composed as she had tried to convince Martha she was. She could be ready for a deep, tranquil sleep.

Could. An elusive word with an indefinite meaning. Of course, she could do all those things if only she hadn't gone to Martha's for dinner. She could if only she hadn't let the memories take hold. She could if only she had never met Dain Maxwell.

Her heart recoiled from the thought. How could she even consider such a possibility? Not ever knowing Dain? Never experiencing the sweet ecstasy of seeing his smile and knowing it was only for her? Never knowing the challenge of his mind or the charm of his laughter or the magic of his lovemaking?

No, she didn't wish they had never met. She couldn't begrudge herself the experience of loving someone so completely. Their marriage had been good, once, and she knew she would live through it all again if given the opportunity.

Amanda slowed her steps. That wasn't true either. She would gladly live through the good times, but under no circumstances would she repeat the last few months. She was never going to hurt like that again. Never.

With the force of a hundred regrets the memories returned. But this time Amanda found no comfort, no pleasure in remembering. Bit by bit the uprooting of her life with Dain came into focus. The first time he'd gone on a weekend business trip and had neglected to call her. The first time he'd spoken affectionately of a friend whose name she didn't recognize. The first time he'd locked himself in the study and then gone on to bed without even saying good night.

Courtesies thoughtlessly neglected, little hurts that went unspoken and unresolved. A gradual undermining of the love that bound them together in understanding. And she had ignored the signs of trouble, pretended that the only problem they faced was conceiving a child.

Amanda tried to stop the memory. She tried to concentrate on the rustling sounds of approaching night, on the full moon just coming into its own as the sunlight faded across the horizon. But she heard the plaintive song of the whippoorwill and she remembered. . . .

She had always wanted children and hadn't considered that wanting didn't necessarily fulfill the desires of the heart. Dain had said he wanted children, too, but he thought they should wait. "We've been married only two years," he had reasoned with her. "You've just begun your career. Let's wait a little longer."

But she had known he didn't really mean it; he just didn't understand how a baby would enrich their marriage. She had known, though, and she hadn't hesitated to cajole him into agreement. It hadn't taken long to convince him or to convince herself that he was as happy with the decision as she.

Amanda kicked blindly at a tuft of grass in her path. Oh, she had thought she knew all the answers then. Everything was just the way she wanted, all was right with her world. She and Dain shared something special, something out of the ordinary, and a baby would be a culmination of that, a fulfillment of their love for each other.

In her mind it had all been so simple, but it hadn't been simple at all.

Like the changing seasons she had changed, and with each barren month came impatience and frustration and a deepening of the insatiable yearning within her. Dain had been understanding at first. He had comforted her, reassured her, sympathized with her during the endless medical tests. He had teased her out of melancholy and made her hope again. He had bribed her laughter with gifts and extra attention. But after a while she couldn't be reassured or teased or bribed and he gradually stopped trying.

It had been fatally easy to misinterpret those early signs

of resentment. She had told herself that because he was a man he couldn't really identify with her desperate longing to bear his child. How could he truly understand that a baby, their baby, would be worth all the waiting and the frustrating disappointment they were facing? She had been foolishly, naively confident that everything would be all right again . . . just as soon as she became pregnant.

The cottage came into view as a welcome interruption to the memories. Amanda opened the door but didn't go inside. Instead, she lingered on the porch, consciously placing her fingers on the railing where she had last seen Dain rest his hand.

She had wished many times that she could go back and erase the mistakes she'd made. If she had only realized then that they needed to talk about their feelings openly and honestly. But the prospect of never being able to give him a child frightened her, made her feel less of a woman, and she couldn't admit that . . . not even to him. So she pretended there was nothing wrong, that the widening gap between them wasn't really there.

A heavy sigh wafted from her throat into the night air as Amanda leaned against the railing. Now she realized how blind she had been. Too obsessed with her desire for motherhood to realize that she was losing Dain.

It was hard to admit that she had been wrong about his feelings from the beginning, but Amanda knew that must have been the case. Dain hadn't really wanted the baby. Oh, she had no doubts that he would have been a loving, responsible father. But he hadn't really wanted or needed the role of parent. And in the end he had gotten his wish.

Somehow that realization hurt more now than it had at the time, but in light of everything that had happened, she couldn't put any other interpretation on it. Dain had resented her longing to become pregnant; he had resented the pregnancy and he had left her to face alone the miracle of birth and the devastation of . . .

Amanda straightened abruptly. Enough. Her dreams were too often full of that nightmarish pain. She would not consciously remember it now. She had made a promise to put the past into perspective and get on with living. And she would do it, one day, one moment at a time.

Today was the only reality. She could manage to enjoy today; she could even make plans for tomorrow, but she wouldn't look too far ahead. Forever was an evanescent promise of starry-eyed lovers. It no longer held any meaning for her.

As a breeze drifted across the water to toss the midnight darkness of her hair, Amanda turned toward the door of the house. Home, she reminded her heart. This was the home she had redecorated as a new beginning. Dain was doing fine without her and the feeling of loss would leave her someday soon. It was only natural that she would experience some loneliness, that she would miss him.

A normal part of breaking away, she thought as she left the memories outside the door. Natural and normal and . . . empty.

CHAPTER FIVE

Dain stepped from the sunlight into the shelter of the building's overhang. He paused there, the indecision tightening across his chest.

Amanda was near. He knew it logically, rationally, of course, because he had come here to find her, but he also knew it in the tense awareness that seemed to bind his every nerve ending. In a few minutes he would see her, look into the blue morning of her eyes and say . . .

God in heaven, what would he say? I miss you? I love you? Come home to me? He could say those things with perfect honesty, but if he did, he would risk an outright rejection. Slow and casual, he must remember that. He hadn't spent the last hellish weeks of waiting only to blow his chances on an impulse.

It was going to take time to gain a foothold in Amanda's life and even longer to reach past her cool façade to the woman he loved. And he had nothing but time to lose.

Dain pushed aside the edges of his suit jacket and thrust

his hands into his trouser pockets. It had been a little over two months since he'd driven away from the cottage, feeling that he wanted to physically smash someone or something, but leaving Amanda to the solitude she wanted. He had meant to give her three full months to think, and he had meant to keep himself too occupied to miss her.

A scornful breath pulled at the tautness in his throat. He hadn't been capable of doing either. Here he was, a good three weeks ahead of his self-imposed limitation, as eager and nervous as a boy in the throes of puppy love. But this malady was far more serious. If he'd had any doubts about the intensity of his love for her, the days since Amanda left him had crushed them out of existence.

How could he have been married to her for so long and never really appreciated what an integral part she played in his every thought? He'd been self-sufficient before she came into his life; he hadn't needed anyone else until Amanda.

Amanda. Even her name was a part of him, a deeply intimate, unconscious part of him. She was constantly with him, in an elusive, intangible way. Ever on the fringes of his mind. Always that empty yearning in his arms.

Had she missed him at all? Martha said Amanda was pining away with missing him, but then you could never depend on what Martha said. She had a way of coloring the truth to suit herself and he had a sinking feeling that Amanda was doing quite well without him despite Martha's assertions to the contrary.

Well, today he would know. He had stayed away as long as he could, longer than he had wanted, but today he was going to see her, hear her voice, and he would know. The prospect filled him with dread, but he had to follow through. He must see her now.

With a cognizant effort to relax, he moved beneath the shadow of the overhang toward the sounds of children playing. A smile tucked into the corners of his mouth as he rounded the building and saw the playground. Sturdy little bodies of all shapes and sizes scampered in every direction, too busy, too secure to pay much attention to him.

Dain watched them with curious fascination, delighting in their energy and enthusiasm. He wondered if his son would have romped so boisterously through childhood. The curve of his smile deepened. Philip Christopher Maxwell would undoubtedly have been the accepted leader of a crew of rowdy preschoolers. Sadness clouded the thought and Dain silently cursed the fate that had robbed his son of that opportunity.

Then, suddenly, the noisy scene before him faded as his body became alert to her nearness. Crazy, of course, but so real that he knew she couldn't be far away. *Amanda. Amanda.*

He saw her then. She stood, graceful and lovely, at the other side of the playground. Turned slightly, she didn't see him immediately, and Dain took advantage to absorb the sight of her into his thirsty soul.

Damn Martha's well-meaning interference! Pining away? Amanda had never looked so glowingly healthy. Her cheeks were flushed with the sun's warmth, her skin more tanned than he ever remembered it being before. Even from where he stood he could tell that her legs were creamy brown and bare beneath her print wraparound skirt. Her lavender knit shirt accentuated the fullness of her breasts and her slender, feminine shape.

Maybe she was a little thinner, he decided. And were those shadows beneath her eyes or just the smudgy line of her lashes? There was a difference in her, although he couldn't put his finger on it. He studied her now with concern, looking for a physical sign that she might have missed him.

Her hair was longer, curving almost to her shoulders. Was she letting it grow again? He hoped so. Over and above the sensual pleasure of touching it, he thought it was a good sign. She had cut it the day after the funeral, had it cropped in a becoming cap of curls. Easier to take care of, she had said, but he'd known better. Amanda had wanted no outward signs of her grief and so she had banished the black mourning veil of hair. When he'd seen the short, wispy curls and realized what she'd done, he had wanted to cry—for her, for himself, and for the comfort she wouldn't allow him to give.

As if conscious of his observation, she lifted a hand to brush at her hair and, for a second, he thought she would turn toward him. Impulsively, he took a few steps closer to her, but if she sensed his presence, she gave no indication, directing her attention instead to a child with a brown, bobbing ponytail and indignant eyes awash with crocodile tears.

"Teacher. Teacher." The child tugged at Amanda's skirt and Dain couldn't resist a brief smile at the small, petulant voice and the way Amanda immediately stooped to make eye contact with her charge. Her response was too soft for Dain to distinguish the words, but his pulse raced as he recognized the throaty tones. Quietly, trying not to attract any notice, he moved closer.

"J-Jason called me names, Teacher." The child sniffed in an obvious plea for sympathy. "He said my name was Mandy Candy and it isn't, Teacher, is it?"

Amanda soothed the imagined injury with a touch of

her hand on the brown ponytail. "No, of course it isn't. Your name is Amanda, just like mine. But would you like to know a secret? I think Jason must like you very much if he calls you Mandy."

"Oh." The tears disappeared like magic and the glimmer of childish understanding took their place. "Jason likes you, Teacher. Does he call you Mandy Candy too?"

Amanda's lips curved in amusement. "No, Jason calls me Mrs. Maxwell or Teacher just as you do. But a long time ago someone used to call me Mandy and it made me feel . . . special."

"Ooohhh." This time understanding sparkled confidently in the child's tiny features. "Did he like you very much?"

Amanda's smile softened with fleeting sadness. "Yes, he liked me very much."

Satisfied, the child nodded and skipped off to play, her ponytail swaying in rhythm to her steps. Amanda rose slowly and turned just enough to look straight at Dain. For a moment in time he thought his heartbeat was clearly audible above the surrounding noise and, in the same instant, he thought his heart must surely have stopped beating.

So lovely. He hadn't forgotten the smallest detail of her face, yet he was captured anew by the familiar piquancy. As a smile dawned in the blue-violet eyes, Dain felt his breath swell and compress in his throat, only to slide effortlessly from his lungs when the smile discovered her lips. Amanda, oh, Amanda.

"Hello, Mandy," he said in a quietly controlled voice. God, did she have any idea how little control he really had? He lightened his tone deliberately. "Or should I say Mandy Candy?"

Her brows arched in whimsical challenge. "Only if you want to get pushed off the jungle gym."

His smile came easily, along with a string of pleasant memories. "Point well taken. I'll steer clear of jungle gyms and nicknames. As I recall, you pushed me off the sailboat once for the same offense."

"Did I really?" she asked softly . . . so softly. "Well, I'm sure you deserved it."

He wondered if nervousness made her voice breathy or if it was just the breeze that altered the sound. "I'm sure I did," he said with husky reminiscence. Dain watched the blush steal into her cheeks and knew she was remembering —just as he was—the intimate teasing that had been so natural then.

Amanda felt the warmth that tinted her cheeks with color and the heated memory that suffused her body with longing for that once-upon-a-time. A time when they had each savored the taste of provocative words and the exchange of secret glances. Wrapped in the wondrous mystery that belonged to all lovers and yet was uniquely their own, they had laughed and learned and loved.

It had been a perfect honeymoon. Two weeks of gentle winds and blue skies, brown eyes and caressing hands, dark hair tangled with blond, his body and hers clothed only in moonlight. Two weeks alone with Dain. A memory that circumstances could not tarnish. A happy memory she could only cherish more with time.

"You're a long way from Baltimore." Amanda tried to assume a casual manner as she silently commanded her gaze away from him. She was staring at him like a lost puppy that finally sees a friendly face. "I certainly never expected to see you here."

"Small world, isn't it?" he offered lightly. "But since I am here, would you like a lift home?"

Her gaze returned to him and she felt unexpectedly cautious and uneasy. Amanda shied from the many possible reasons for his sudden appearance and settled on the most obvious and least important. "Let me guess," she said with a slight shake of her head. "Mr. MacGregor had an attack of posion ivy or something equally disabling and Martha twisted your arm until you cried 'Chauffeur.' Right?"

"Now, how did you know?" Dain closed the gap between them with two steps. "Martha thought she'd invented the perfect alibi. Poor MacGregor. She's probably soaked him in anti-itch cream just for the sake of authenticity."

"Poor MacGregor, nothing. He's never done anything Martha wanted him to do and I'm sure he hasn't started now. I'm sorry, though, that Martha coerced you into coming for me."

"My pleasure, Amanda. Besides, there are some things I need to discuss with you."

Her heart sank in slow degrees to her toes. Things to discuss. She imagined the rustle of crisp legal-size papers and knew what he wanted to discuss. With a blind glance at her watch, Amanda nodded agreement. "I'll be ready to leave in twenty minutes." Her hand fidgeted with the hair at her nape. Had she seemed too eager? Did he recognize how very glad she was to see him? Did he know how very hard it was to pretend she was only pleasantly surprised?

"My car's in the shop for a tune-up," she said, although she knew it was a pointless explanation. "That's why Mr. MacGregor was chauffeuring me today."

"I know. Martha told me." Dain smoothed the striped fabric of his tie as his gaze strayed past Amanda to the play equipment behind her. "If it's all right, I'll wait for you here." A glint of humor shaded the set of his mouth. "You never know what sort of tip you'll pick up when you hang around the jungle gym."

"Hang around? Figuratively speaking, I hope?"

The familiar tilt of his head and his leisurely smile caught at her heart's composure. "I'm afraid so. Even if I had the energy, I doubt I could compete with those sturdy little guys." He nodded toward the preschoolers climbing busily on the bars. Amanda watched as ever so slowly his smile dimmed, clouded by impotent wishes that she understood all too well. "Does it bother you to work here, Amanda?" he asked, his eyes seeking empathy in hers.

Consciously, she looked away as her heart closed over the feelings his words evoked and shielded them from exposure. She lifted a hand to her hair and then touched her lips, discovering the practiced curve was already in place.

"No, of course not," she answered in crisp, casual misinterpretation. "I enjoy every minute. There's a lot to learn though. A lot more to good child care than most people realize. And speaking of child care, I'd better take my class inside and get them ready to go home. When I'm through for the day, I'll meet you at the car—the Mercedes?" At his nod she turned her attention to calling her class together and then walked toward the building with the children following at her heels.

Once inside, Amanda had little time to think about Dain or to dwell on the reason for his unexpected appearance, but his nearness enveloped her in a misty blend of pleasure and pain. She passed out papers and paintings with a steady hand, patiently answered a thousand questions, and made sure each child left with the right parent. She exchanged laughing comments with Susan, the head teacher of the preschool class, as they tidied the room. It seemed like hours to Amanda before she could finally slip from the building and into the sunshine.

Her gaze scanned the street for Dain's car as she hesitated just outside the door. She found the Mercedes . . . and Dain. With arms folded across his chest, he leaned against the front fender. His suit jacket stretched taut over his shoulders and his hair was disheveled by the wind. Amanda thought how she had often played the wind's ally and tousled his hair with teasing fingers. Only sometimes she hadn't been teasing—she had been breathlessly, passionately serious.

She stood for just a moment, watching him, giving herself time to notice all the details she hadn't forgotten and yet hadn't been able to clearly recall either. With the perspective of several weeks, Amanda decided he had lost some weight and gained an enviable tan. It was purely conjecture on her part, considering the three-piece summer suit he wore, and she wished he were dressed in cutoffs and nothing more.

Her gaze lowered to sinewy legs covered by lightweight khaki trousers, and then lifted to the glimpse of beige shirt front that concealed his lean stomach and sunkissed skin. Yes, she definitely preferred Dain in cutoffs—or in nothing at all.

It was an immodest thought that wouldn't have occurred to her a few weeks ago, but Amanda didn't chase it away. There wasn't anything wrong in admiring the special qualities that made a man attractive, was there?

Men were notorious for quoting and misquoting those same sentiments about women, so why should she feel embarrassed?

Self-consciously she shifted the strap of her purse on her shoulder and drew a deep breath. Dain wasn't just a man she found attractive. He was her estranged husband and he had come to discuss their divorce. Amanda sighed. She had no business thinking of Dain as attractive, whether he was dressed immodestly or not.

With an attempt at swallowing her nervous apprehension, she walked toward him and stopped a few feet away. "Dain? I'm ready to leave now."

He turned his head and the look in his eyes was dark and distant, as if he'd been lost in thought and had been brought reluctantly back to reality. Slowly he straightened and moved to open the car door for her. She slid onto the seat and tried to quell the familiar sense of belonging in the place next to Dain. When he got in beside her and started the car, Amanda wondered how something that felt right could also feel very wrong.

"Would you like to stop somewhere for a drink?" Dain glanced in her direction. "Or we could have dinner if you'd like."

"No," Amanda answered too quickly. "I'm not hungry. Or thirsty. Thanks anyway." She clasped her hands and smiled stiffly at the windshield. How she hated being so conscious of every word she spoke and every movement she made. Dain appeared cool, calm, and indifferent to the tense awareness that coursed her veins with a disconcerting static effect.

She wanted the trip to be over. She wanted it to continue. Contradictions sparked in her mind and wound into a tangle of nerves. "What did you need to discuss with me?" she asked at last, waiting, half-afraid to hear his reply.

Dain reached for the inside pocket of his jacket, but his hand came out empty. With a slight frown he patted the outside pockets and then his shirt pocket. "Damn. I must have forgotten. . . ." His cheeks creased with a rueful grimace. "I brought—intended to bring—the inventory to go over with you."

"Inventory?" Amanda asked, glancing at him cautiously.

"The list of household furnishings and personal items that have to be divided in the settlement." His brows arched as if he were surprised she had asked. "Your attorney's requested it several times, but I've just been too busy with the Reichmann account to get it done before now. I hope the delay hasn't caused you any problem."

"Oh, no." Amanda felt the rough assessment of his eyes on her, but she kept the stiff smile firmly in place. She vaguely remembered her attorney asking her about an inventory and she had wondered why the divorce proceedings were taking such a long time, why the court date for the final decree had not been set. She had simply signed the petition papers and had closed her mind to the details until she was forced to face them—like now. "I guess this means another delay, though, since you forgot to bring it with you." Something about the idea didn't quite fit and her gaze turned to him curiously. "Funny. It isn't like you to forget, Dain."

His eyes met hers for an infinite second. "But then I don't have you around to remind me, do I, Amanda?" Before she had a chance to consider the meaning of his words or the throaty tone of his voice, Dain lifted his shoulder in a shrug. "We don't have to have the list. I suppose we could just talk about the few things I wasn't sure what to do with."

Amanda mentally braced herself. "Such as?"

"The grandfather clock, for one. I know it was a wedding gift from my parents, but you picked it out. And then there's the landscape we bought in the Bahamas. You always were especially fond of that painting."

"Those things go with the house, Dain. You should keep them."

"I'm thinking of selling the house."

"Oh." Her heart flinched at the idea and a sliver of resentment pricked her calm veneer, but she maintained control of her voice. "I guess that is the sensible thing to do."

Dain merely smiled, his attention on slowing the Mercedes at an intersection. "Then," he continued smoothly as if he hadn't just blithely dismissed all the thought, effort, and fun they'd had in planning that house, "there's also a problem about the custody of our suit of armor. I know Martha thought it a wonderful addition to the front hall, but I'm not sure a potential buyer would agree. Do you think she could be blackmailed into taking the thing back?"

Amanda laughed despite the knot that pressed painfully against her throat. "Martha wouldn't take it on a bet. Maybe the museum?"

"Or the city dump. It isn't exactly a museum piece, you know."

"No, I suppose it isn't." She hated the image of the suit of armor lying rusted on a pile of garbage. It had never really fit in with the decor of the house, but it was an interesting conversation piece. Still, she had no place for the armor, and if Dain sold the house, what could she do?

Amanda felt a pang of guilt, as if she had betrayed a friend, and her stomach muscles contracted with another, more intense feeling of resentment.

She didn't want to talk about the dismantling of their home. Dain knew how stupidly sentimental she could be. Why didn't he just do whatever he wanted with the house and its contents? That was what she'd intended for him to do. She'd even informed her attorney that whatever Dain decided was fine with her, hoping the message would be transmitted through legal channels. Obviously, it had gone astray.

Amanda turned toward Dain and caught him watching her closely, but in an instant the serious look vanished from his eyes. He laughed softly. A laugh she remembered well, and yet, it didn't sound quite as she remembered.

"It really wasn't very nice of you, Amanda, to leave the marlin with me. You know how it hurt my pride when you caught the damned fish after I invested two days and a small fortune on deep-sea fishing."

She had accused him of pouting for days, but actually he had been proud of her catch and insisted on having it mounted. Amanda hadn't thought of that day in a very long time and the memory now was bittersweet fuel for her irritation. Damn! Why had he forgotten that list? She could have viewed a written inventory of their possessions dispassionately, without remembering all the circumstances that made each possession special to her.

"You can keep the fish," she stated briskly. "And the painting and the clock and the armor. I have no place for them. I—I have all that I need, Dain. Whatever you decide is fine. Fine." She felt him watching her again, but refused to acknowledge his curious look.

"Are you sure, Amanda? I wouldn't want to get rid of

something and then have you asking about it later. That's the reason for the inventory, so that there's no question about—"

"I know the reason, Dain," she snapped, the tension building inside her. "I promise that I won't question your integrity, now or later on. My attorney explained the settlement to me. It seems fair, more than fair, so please, do whatever you want with the house and the things in it. I don't need to know what you do with them."

There was a moment's pause and then he said quietly, "But I want you to know, Amanda."

Her control slipped and she faced him angrily. "I don't care. Do you hear me, Dain? I don't want to know. I don't need to know. And I don't care!" On a ragged breath she reined in her unleashed emotions and felt them fade as rapidly as they had come. Her gaze slipped from beneath her downcast lashes to gauge his reaction. Oddly, he didn't appear surprised. His lips curved, not in a smile, but in a satisfied line.

"Almost home," he announced as they drove past the sweeping driveway of Martha's house and turned onto the road that led to the cottage. "Martha says you've done wonders with the place, Amanda. Of course, she thinks you're a natural wonder no matter what you do." Within a few minutes Dain had parked the Mercedes and shifted to slide his arm along the back of the seat. "Well, are you going to invite me in?"

Amanda tensed, but whether it was because of his question or because of his large hand that lay so very close to her shoulder, she wasn't sure. She eyed him thoughtfully. "Do you want to see the 'wonders' I've done with the place for yourself?"

"Of course. You didn't really think I'd take Martha's

word for it, did you?" He grinned as he loosened the knot of his tie. "What kind of wonders can you do with a little ice, some water, and a teabag?"

"Iced tea?"

"Damn! That's a clever idea, Amanda. Let's try it."

She tried to frown away his good humor, but found herself smiling an invitation instead. "All right. Come on."

His fingers made an airy brush stroke against her hair and along the curve of her cheek. "You always did know just how to entice me into accepting your invitations, didn't you?"

"It was never really very difficult, Dain," she said, responding naturally to his teasing. "You always were . . . easy."

Dark gold brows lifted as a slow smile tugged at his mouth—and at her heart. "Only for you, Amanda."

Her breath suspended, she stared into his eyes for the space of a heartbeat. He made a slight movement toward her and, fearful that he might touch her again in that casual, yet familiar way, Amanda's hand found the handle and opened the door. "Let's go," she said as she stepped from the car. "You'll be my first guest since the decorating was finished."

She waited for him to join her before she walked up the porch steps and unlocked the front door. It was difficult to control the impulse to chatter aimlessly, but she knew Dain would recognize her nervousness if she did. Inside, Amanda directed him to wander about the house at will while she made some tea. She wanted to follow at his heels, watching his face for signs of approval. Ever since she'd finished the redecorating, she'd wished he could see the house, had wanted to know his opinion, hear him say he liked what she'd done. So why had she denied herself the satisfaction?

Because she was as tense as a string quartet. That was why. In the kitchen Amanda filled the kettle and set the water on to boil, wondering all the while what Dain was thinking—about the house, about her job, about her. Seeing him at the center had been almost like a scene from an old movie. Unexpected and yet something within her had known that one day she would turn around and see him there. She had felt—how had she felt? Surprised? Yes. Curious? A little. Nervous? Definitely. Glad? More than she wanted to admit.

But none of those reactions were particularly revealing. Old habits didn't die overnight and emotions were often nothing more than a conditioned response. Still, she knew that wasn't what bothered her.

Amanda stared for a long time at the beads of sweat forming on the kettle before she allowed the answer to form in her thoughts. It was the awareness. The tight play of her breathing, the erratic cadence of her pulse, the ever-present alert to his movements. The awareness. It practically vibrated through her each time he was near. She hadn't experienced that kind of physical reaction in a very long time. It was unsettling to feel it now, now when there was nothing left but memories.

"Very nice, Amanda." Dain entered the kitchen, startling her from her contemplation and bringing her full attention to him. His gaze evaluated the changes she'd made in the room before focusing on her. "I hardly recognized the cottage beneath the fresh touch of your talent. It isn't your usual style, but I like it. It's soft and relaxing and . . ." He hesitated, searching for the word. "Waiting."

Immediately, Amanda turned back to the now whistling kettle and busied her hands with making tea. He had so quickly summed up her own feelings about the redecorating of the cottage. *Waiting.* Would it ever come to an end?

Dain shrugged out of his jacket and tossed it on the back of a chair before he moved to lean against the counter beside her. "You know, Amanda, I think you need the four-poster in the bedroom upstairs. It would look perfect here."

The four-poster? The bed she'd shared with Dain? How could he even suggest it? "No. I don't think so. It's just too big. I doubt it would even fit through the door."

"Hmmm." He watched silently while she set the tea aside to brew, then he laughed suddenly. A quiet, reminiscent laugh. "I'll never forget the look on your face the first time you saw that bed or the way you insisted you'd never lay a finger on it, much less sleep there." A throaty chuckle drifted into the air between them. "I guess it was a little indecent before we stripped the paint and refinished it."

"Indecent?" Amanda pushed a wayward tendril of hair from her face. "Dain Maxwell, you know good and well the pictures painted on that bed were positively obscene. I don't know how you ever convinced me it was a priceless antique awaiting my transforming touch."

"I believe I told you a story about the princess who kissed a frog."

Amanda laughed with the recollection. "That wasn't the only fairy tale you concocted. Wasn't there a line about exorcising ghosts and starting new traditions?"

He lifted a hand in rueful concession. "I had to think of some way to get you into that bed."

"It would have been much simpler to get another bed," she observed dryly.

"Yes, well, I may be easy, Amanda, but I'm never simple. Besides, that line worked like a charm—once." His gaze fell slowly, almost reluctantly to her mouth and her heart began an uneven pounding. "I wonder," he whispered to the curve of her lips, "I wonder what would happen if I tried that line now."

"Nothing." She lifted her chin to emphasize her point in case he should doubt her. "I don't believe in fairy tales anymore."

"I know." His eyes found hers and locked her into their dark intensity. "What *do* you believe in, Amanda? Do you believe we shared something special? Do you believe our marriage was good?"

"Yes. Once upon a time." She wanted to escape his questioning gaze, but he held her by a bond of memory and she couldn't look away. "I—Dain, I'm sorry." Such a meaningless phrase, she thought. An apology without purpose. Pointless, yet somehow necessary. A way of reaching out to him and the past they had shared.

But Dain didn't understand. She saw it in his face, in the subtle straightening of his shoulders, long before she heard it in his deep sigh. "Don't apologize, Amanda. I shouldn't have . . ." He broke the visual contact and stared moodily at the wall. "We're halfway to a divorce decree and I can't stop remembering. I should have forgotten by now, but little things keep reminding me."

A sadly inadequate smile was the only response she could make, but she understood. Oh, yes, she understood.

"Do you know what I thought of the other day, Amanda?" He leaned back and braced an elbow on the countertop, a deceptively relaxed pose because she could sense the tension in him. "Do you remember the Sunday we drove into Baltimore and windowshopped? It was only a week or so after you had gotten out of the hospital after the tests."

Amanda drew back, not wanting to remember, but unable to stop the images that flooded her mind.

"It was snowing just a little and we walked for a long time. I was afraid you would get too tired, but you laughed at me for worrying. We talked a lot that day. I can't remember about what, but I know we talked. And then you started to cry. All of a sudden. And I didn't know what to do, so I put my arms around you and held you. Right in the middle of downtown Baltimore." His voice lowered to a strained whisper. "Do you remember that, Amanda?"

Remember? Oh, God, of course I remember. Dain had been so tender. And she hadn't been able to explain her tears. She hadn't been able to do anything except cry. But he had held her tight against him, comforting, protecting, until the noise around her, and in her, had faded to the steady sound of his heartbeat and the soft feel of snowflakes on her cheek. *Remember?* It had been the single most perfect moment in her life. "Yes," she breathed out the admission. "Yes, I remember."

Abruptly, Amanda spun away from the memory and jerked open a cabinet door, relieved to see that it was actually the right one. She set two glasses on the counter and tried to think what she should do next. Ice. She should put ice into the glasses and then tea. Her hand went automatically to the teapot.

"Maybe," Dain said pensively, "I remember that day so clearly because it's the last time I ever saw you cry."

Stillness closed over her like the snow on that long-ago day and she turned to him, intending to dispel the mood with a word. But she met his gaze and the awareness caught her. It whirled from her thoughts to Dain and she saw it flicker and then kindle to flame in his eyes.

With the swift ferocity of a summer storm Amanda was swept into a tempest of memories of all the times she had lain in his arms, burning with his touch, with her own desire and with the fierce need to love him. All those memories, and their accompanying emotions, streaked through her and left her weak. She trembled, helpless to stop her hand from reaching to touch his face.

His skin felt roughly soft beneath her palm and soothed her confused thoughts with its familiarity. When he moved ever so slowly to press his lips against the hollow of her wrist, it seemed natural to step closer to his warmth. And he was warm. As his arms slipped around her, she nestled into his embrace and the warm memories she found there.

Dain. She had almost forgotten how nice it felt to be held and touched by him. Just by closing her eyes she could summon the image of his body, stripped of all but her admiring gaze and caressing hands. She had delighted in touching him, had reveled with the delicious vanity of knowing he responded to her, and only to her. He was her mate, her lover, belonging to her in the same intimate, irrevocable way she belonged to him.

It had been nice to belong to Dain in that special way. And Amanda wanted to belong to him again, just for a little while. Just until the loneliness subsided a bit.

"Amanda?" His fingers forced up her chin and made her face the question in his eyes, made her acknowledge that she wanted more than his arms around her. God, she wanted so much more. She wanted to taste him, wanted to know the mindless ecstasy of his possession. She wanted to assuage the emptiness inside her. She wanted to feel again, to love him just once more.

Her body moved to secure the wish of her heart. Lifting her lips to his, she let her hands glide over his chest and around his neck. Slowly, lingeringly, she drew his head down until his breath mingled with hers and filled her with quivering expectancy. It had been so long . . . so very long.

Her thick lashes drifted down to conceal from her view the hesitancy she felt in him. *Love me, Dain,* her heart whispered. *Pretend if you must, but please, for this one moment, this tiny fragment of time, please, love me again.*

Her lips trembled with a sigh that Dain captured with a windsoft kiss. A kiss that echoed through her like a gentle lullaby and crescendoed into a heady melody of desire. She couldn't get close enough, couldn't get warm enough. With a husky moan she pressed against his hard thigh, molding herself to fit and meld into his body's symmetry.

His arms tightened as he stroked her back in a sensual sweep from shoulder to hip. Lingering there, his fingers compelled her even closer until the pulsating feel of his heartbeat throbbed inside her. The tremulous rhythm began an upward spiral and changed the texture of the kiss that still claimed her.

From tenderly mobile to roughly demanding, his lips seared her with their touch, fusing past and present into an exhilarating now. As he ran the tip of his tongue along the inner curve of her mouth, she opened to the searching invader. Feverish shivers of déjà vu cascaded her spine and Amanda pushed against him in an effort to satisfy the craving within her.

Dain's hands found her waist and half-lifted, half-pulled her against him. His fingers were urgent and almost rough in their quest to tug her shirt free. Then he discovered the knot of her wraparound skirt and shifted his attention there.

Amanda felt it come undone and the sliding of the material as it fell. Something cautioned her that she should stop the skirt from dropping away, but she couldn't think why. Dain had undressed her many times before . . . and she had undressed him.

Her fingers went to the buttons of his shirt as his fingers pushed up the knit top, making tantalizing strokes against her skin until he reached her breasts. She pulled back from his kiss then, arching her neck to invite his plunder. A thrill vibrated in the core of her being as his lips accepted the invitation and moved in erotic circles along her neck.

The stimulating caress of his thumb brought a nipple to a throbbing hardness. Her breasts lifted and strained toward him, demanding a more complete mastery. Amanda parted his shirt and slid her hands inside to tangle and tease the cloud of hair on his chest. It was an incredibly alive feeling to be touching him like this . . . and to be touched by him. God, she felt so good.

His head dipped lower as his tongue tasted the rosy peak of her desire. In hungered response her hands went to the belt at his waist and stopped. Something wasn't right. Dain never wore a belt with cutoffs. The thought rippled through the hazy mist of memories and rent the cushion of unreality that had surrounded her. This wasn't once upon a time. It was now, and they were getting a divorce.

The stillness began a steady rise, cooling the heat of desire with reason. How had she allowed herself to be trapped by the past? Loneliness wasn't an excuse. Neither were the empty nights of remembering. She owed him an apology, even if she couldn't begin to explain or excuse her behavior.

"Dain." It was a painful breath that barely warmed her lips in passing, but she waited for him to hear.

He heard long before she breathed out his name. He had known by her stillness, by the slow withdrawal of her spirit even as her body still clung to his. He tightened his arms around her as if he could stop her retreat, but he knew it was a futile gesture. Amanda had left him . . . again.

He straightened, releasing her by degrees, schooling his features to a calm façade that matched her composure. Not by the flicker of an eyelash would he reveal the aching frustration inside him. He had known better, had warned himself not to touch her but, for just a moment, he had thought she needed him. And he had wanted so desperately to believe that she did.

Why was he putting himself through this slow agony? Why couldn't he leave her now and never look back? It was what any sensible, sane man would do. But as he watched her bend to lift her skirt from the floor and wrap it around her slender hips with a quiet dignity, he knew he wouldn't give up. Amanda had to stop running away from her emotions sometime. Sometime she would have to face all the feelings she had hidden from her heart. Sometime she would cry. And when she did, he would be there to hold her.

She looked up and he tried to reassure her with a smile, but he couldn't be sure his attempt was recognizable. "Dain," she said in a raspy whisper. "I'm sorry that hap—"

"Don't." He cut through her words with a shake of his head. How could he bear to hear her apologize for some-

103

thing that he had wanted, needed so badly? He inhaled a deep, shaky breath and tried another smile to soften the brusqueness of his voice. "I think I'll skip the iced tea, Amanda. I'm not really thirsty anymore."

She nodded, her blue eyes regarding him with shadowy regret.

"Are you going to the reception for Jim Barnett next month?" Dain asked, not sure where the thought had come from but grateful for the impersonal tone that might, just might, erase the look in her eyes. "He's made some elaborate plans for his retirement and I know he'll be disappointed if you aren't at the party."

The curve of her lips was brief. "I wouldn't want to disappoint Jim, but I don't know. It would be the first time I've gone to something like that without—"

The rest of the thought went unspoken, but Dain finished it in his mind. *Without you.* That was what she had almost said and he wished he could ask her to go with him. But she would only refuse. If she came to the reception at all, it would be alone. "Maybe I'll see you there," he offered as casually as he could.

"Maybe."

Her voice was crisp now, almost curt, and Dain knew there was no point in lingering. He toyed with the idea of mentioning the inventory list again, but decided she had heard the word *divorce* enough for one day. He didn't want her to begin questioning the delays that he and Jerry had worked so hard to achieve.

With one last, lingering look at her, he said good-bye and walked away from the house. In the car he curled his hands around the steering wheel, steadying his resolve to leave. One quick twist of the key and he would be on his way. He had seen Amanda, talked with her, touched her.

It was more than he had hoped for, but less than he'd wanted. Still, it was a start. His fingers found the key and gave it a twist. The Mercedes purred to life and, in a matter of seconds, he was driving away from the cottage, away from Amanda and into a hot, summer evening.

Dain noted the heat with a frown. As far as he was concerned, it was already cold, gray winter.

CHAPTER SIX

"Amanda!" The call came above the muted conversation in the crowded room.

Amanda tracked the sound with her gaze, tilting her head to the side so she could see around the elderly couple in front of her. She lifted a hand to answer Meg's wave and waited patiently for the couple to move through the reception line ahead of her. The taffeta fabric of her dress made a lazy swish against her legs as she stepped forward to offer congratulations to Jim Barnett.

His hefty handshake and disarming smile almost concealed the expectant glance he tossed, and then recovered, when he realized the person behind her in line was not Dain. It was a simple, split-second mistake, but Amanda caught it and wished that she had stayed home.

She moved on after a brief exchange with the guest of honor and stopped to take a glass of punch before walking toward the terrace doors where Meg waited. "Hi," Amanda said, feeling a little awkward and out of place despite their longstanding friendship. "You look gorgeous tonight. Is that a new dress?"

Meg looked down as if she couldn't remember what she was wearing. Her gaze went from the slim lines of her black sarong to Amanda's dress. Amanda smiled at her friend's wide-eyed expression, knowing the red taffeta with its softly flared skirt and deep, rounded neckline was unusual and certainly eye-catching. She had bought it for that very reason.

It had been difficult to commit herself to coming to the reception in the first place, but once committed, Amanda had decided she needed a little extra confidence. So she'd shopped for the right dress. The vivid color made her feel somewhat flashy, but she knew that, for all its brightness, the dress was deliciously feminine and extremely flattering, a much-needed ego builder for the evening ahead.

Meg wrinkled her nose. "Considering that your dress positively shouts 'Paris designer,' Amanda, you don't know how much I'd like to say I dug this old rag out of the closet. However, I'll try to be gracious and accept wallflower status next to your 'rose.'"

Amanda laughed softly. "Now, Meg, is that a subtle way of suggesting I help you prop up the wall?"

"Not a chance of that," Meg said with a shake of her head. "As soon as Jerry gets through wiping the fog from his glasses, he's going to ask you to dance. I know that look, Amanda, and if I were you, I'd refuse."

Glancing toward Meg's husband, Amanda leaned forward. "Are you going to tell me why I shouldn't dance with such an attractive man?"

Meg's gaze went lovingly to the brown-haired, blue-eyed Jerry. "He really is attractive, isn't he? If I weren't already married . . ." The thought ended on a sigh.

"But you are married," Amanda reminded her, "to him."

"I know." Meg turned her secret smile toward Amanda. "That's what makes it so nice."

It was a sentiment Amanda could identify with—she had often felt the same way about Dain. Many times, in a roomful of people, she had thought her husband the most attractive, most desirable man present. And it had been nice, indescribably so, to exchange a look, a touch, and to know that not another person could interpret the quiet communion of their thoughts.

A whispery chill of isolation slid down her back. How odd it seemed to feel so alone in a familiar crowd. Truly alone. She was no longer a part of a comfortable twosome, and the realization wedged tightly in her throat.

"Amanda, you look great!" Jerry presented the compliment to Amanda as he absently handed Meg a glass of punch. "Would you like to dance?" He pushed his dark-framed glasses into place with a jab of his index finger and smiled at Meg. "You don't mind if Amanda and I take a turn around the floor, do you?"

"Of course not," Meg answered sweetly. "I'll just wait here and lean firmly against the wall."

"That's a good idea. I'd hate for it to fall." Jerry grinned and leaned forward to kiss Meg's cheek. "Here, while you're supporting the wall, hold Amanda's punch, would you?" Smoothly, he took Amanda's cup from her hand and placed it in Meg's. "We'll be right back. Come on, Amanda, let me show you what a mean jitterbug I can do."

"*Jitterbug?*" As Jerry guided her away, Amanda mouthed the word to Meg, but met only a mischievous wink.

"I did try to warn you," Meg said, and with an innocent shrug, she turned to speak to another guest.

Amanda followed Jerry's lead, although she wasn't at all sure she wanted to dance. She felt uncomfortable despite the fact that he didn't even come close to doing the jitterbug.

"You really do look great tonight, Amanda." Jerry drew back to smile at her with the ease of long acquaintance. "It's good to see you. The neighborhood get-togethers haven't been the same without you and . . ."

Dain. Amanda disguised the sigh that rose to her lips and decided to face the issue squarely. There was no point in avoiding the mere mention of his name. She returned Jerry's smile. "Doesn't Dain join you at the get-togethers? He is still part of the neighborhood, you know."

"We don't see him often, but it isn't for lack of invitations. Everyone is rallying around—" Jerry broke off the sentence. "I mean, we're all hoping, of course, that—"

This time Amanda broke through the words. "It's all right, Jerry. I realize this is an awkward situation." Awkward? It was awful, and she wished again that she were anywhere else but here, among familiar strangers who cared about her. She cleared her throat to make room for some confidence. "As soon as the divorce is final, it will be easier for everyone. I've wondered, Jerry, why it's taking so long. My attorney only mumbles some legal jabberwocky about court appearances and delays. Isn't there something we can do to speed things along?"

Jerry concentrated on making a neat turn and adding an interesting shuffle to his dance step. "These things take time, Amanda. Are you really in that much of a hurry? Have you met someone else?"

"No," she snapped, astonished that he could even give

the thought a second's consideration. "And I'm not in a hurry. I'd just like to have the matter settled."

"It is settled, isn't it? A piece of paper doesn't make you divorced any more than a marriage license automatically makes you married. You and Dain seem to have everything worked out to your mutual satisfaction, so I don't see any reason to rush the final decree."

"I suppose there isn't any particular reason, but I do think it's better to—"

"Good. It probably won't take more than another month or so, Amanda." He twirled her once more around a corner of the tiny dance floor as the music swayed toward an ending. "You realize, don't you, that I'm honor-bound to make at least one effort to get you and Dain to talk to each other and try to work out your problems. It's a matter of ethics, you understand."

Amanda let a breath of impatience escape. "Jerry, I appreciate your concern, but even I know that isn't necessary. Besides, my attorney hasn't said anything about an attempt at reconciliation, by his instigation or by yours."

"Can I help it if you chose an unethical lawyer?" Jerry shrugged as they turned in unison to make their way back to Meg. "Ethics aside, Amanda, this divorce is all wrong. You and Dain belong together."

Pressing her lips into a firm line, Amanda ran a hand beneath the loose curls at her nape. She should have avoided any and all mention of Dain. It was easy to see that now that Jerry's reticence to broach the subject of the divorce had yielded to good-intentioned interference. "That's really a matter of opinion," Amanda said in a tone designed to close the conversation.

Jerry stopped her progress across the room with a touch

110

of his hand on her arm. "What would you say if I told you that Dain shares my opinion?"

With a deep, heartfelt sigh, Amanda turned around to face Jerry once more. "I'd say you're a dear friend, Jerry, but please don't push for a reconciliation. It isn't going to happen and it can only strain your friendship with Dain."

Jerry's frown was ruefully cheerful. "In words that even a lawyer can understand, mind your own business."

"Well put." She smiled then, and together they walked to where Meg stood talking with several friends. Amanda exchanged greetings with Bob and Terri Henderson and another couple whom she knew only slightly. Meg's smile seemed a little forced and it took Amanda a full minute to guess the reason.

Dain had arrived. Amanda couldn't see him yet, but the looks that strayed past her shoulder and then jerked guiltily back to her were evidence enough. The trivial conversation within the group came in fits and starts and was as obvious as the clumsy silences between.

Amanda curled her fingers into the crisp fabric of her dress, knowing that she was the cause of the unnatural stiltedness. The tension in the air around her pulled and snapped at her nerves as Meg began talking about a planned trip to Cancún.

Let them talk, Amanda thought. Let them discuss vacations or Mexico or any number of other amiable topics. She had nothing to say. Her intangible separation from this group of friends was as inexplicable as it was true. She was separated from them by the simple fact that she and Dain were in the same room, but were not together. And she was separated from Dain by a width of several feet and a hundred questions that would never be asked or answered.

The distance to him was easily and unexpectedly bridged by her all-too-eager gaze. Her breathing wavered unevenly as, at the same instant, he turned to look in her direction. It was unsettling to meet his dark eyes across the crowded room and Amanda stood staring, unable to fathom the clouded emotions skimming through her senses.

It was almost like seeing him for the first time, almost as if the seconds hung suspended and then spun backward to the moment she had seen him as a stranger and yet had felt her heart stir with recognition. They had stood then, as they did now, locked in a visual embrace, each uncertain of the other, but aware of the silent communication between them.

Damn! Amanda forced her gaze away and compelled her thoughts to reality. No matter how intimately she had once known him, Dain was now a stranger to her heart and there was no communication between them, silent or otherwise.

It just wasn't fair that in one brief look she had noticed so many things about him—the new, slightly different style of his hair, the courtly smile that barely tipped his lips. His white jacket and black slacks might have seemed out of place on any other man, but they looked distinctive and very right on Dain. The masculine grace that defined his every movement remained clear in her mind. Even now she thought him the most attractive, most desirable man in the room, and her pulse raced with ambivalent emotions.

"Will you be able to come?" Terri asked, jarring Amanda back to the conversation.

Glancing to Meg for a clue to the question, Amanda lifted her hand in a noncommittal gesture. "I'm not sure.

Can I let you know later?" With a desperate hope that her answer made sense, she smiled weakly and decided to leave as soon as she politely could.

"It sounds like fun, Amanda." Meg's lifted eyebrow and tone of voice warned that "it" really didn't sound like fun at all. "I'm sure you'll enjoy meeting Terri's brother."

"I know you'll like him," Terri agreed immediately. "And he'll like you. I'll just be careful not to mention to him that you're coming. He has this crazy superstition about blind dates."

Amanda stiffened with the panicky impulse to laugh. "That's very—thoughtful of you, Terri, but I'm afraid I'll have to refuse. I'm superstitious myself. So you see, it just wouldn't work out." Her voice faltered at the asinine excuse, and she wondered what in heaven's name she was doing. "What did you do with my punch, Meg? Oh, never mind, I'll get some more." With an abrupt turn Amanda left her friends to wonder at her odd behavior.

At the refreshment bar she asked for a drink and told herself that it would be rude to leave now. She could maintain her composure for another half-hour, couldn't she? Of course she could, as long as no one else suggested a blind date. The idea sent a repulsive shiver through her. How could Terri—how could anyone—believe she would want a date, whether he was blind or could see in the dark?

With a grimace of distaste at the adolescent pun, Amanda turned to accept the scotch and water with a gracious, if somewhat artificial smile. As she moved toward the open terrace doors, she decided it had been at least seven years since she'd had a "date," and even then it had been with Dain.

She couldn't remember the last time she'd gone out with

another man. And she certainly had no desire to do so now. Date. God, even the word sounded juvenile.

On the terrace she sought a secluded corner and sipped at the drink in her hand. Perhaps it was a good thing she had come to the reception. At least now she knew that a divorce changed everything, even old friendships. Although no one had meant for it to happen, the pattern of easy camaraderie had been broken and Amanda knew that over a period of time she would lose contact with most of the people here tonight.

She could accept that, Amanda thought. What bothered her was the nagging possibility that Dain would continue to be a part of this circle of friends, and that one day her place in the group would be taken by someone else—someone who would also take her place in Dain's life. She shivered suddenly and rubbed her arm as if there were a chill in the air.

Too late. The words blew in a cool whisper through her mind. Too late for regrets. Too late to go back. Too late to consider the ever-widening ripple of consequences. Too late. Too late.

Amanda pivoted to escape the voice of reason and froze at the sight of Dain, who stood just outside the doorway watching her. Slowly, hesitantly, his lips curved a greeting as he took the few steps to her side.

"Hello, Amanda." The deep resonance of her name echoed within her and warmed her like the melody of an old song. "I'm glad you decided to come," he said. "Are you enjoying the party?"

It was too much trouble to compose a lie and, besides, this was Dain—the one person in the room with whom it was unnecessary to pretend. She sipped her drink and then

114

offered a wry smile. "If I were enjoying the party, do you think I'd be hiding in a dark corner of the terrace?"

His soft laughter was soothing. "You shouldn't try to hide anywhere in that dress. I like it very much, but it's a little too conspicuous to blend in with the scenery." He paused and his gaze slid to her neckline, then traced a lingering path back to her face. "You're very beautiful, Amanda, even in a dark corner."

Embarrassed by the compliment, Amanda swept him a curtsy. "Thank you, kind sir," she quipped. "And may I say that you look strikingly handsome tonight yourself."

He bowed to acknowledge her tribute and then stepped closer, leaning toward her as if he were about to share a secret. "Is there a good reason why two such attractive people are hiding on the terrace?"

Amanda relaxed a little, her senses tingling with the deliciously familiar scent of his cologne. "Of course," she answered in a whisper. "Think what people would say if we were seen together."

"Ah, too much rare beauty might be overwhelming for such an august gathering, is that it?"

His breath was a warm caress against her cheek and it occurred to her that if she turned her head just a fraction of an inch, their lips would touch. She made a low sound that resembled a breathy laugh. "It's your sense of humor that's overwhelming, Dain."

"You always did have a keen appreciation for my finer qualities, Amanda. Maybe that's why I like you." He moved away from her and leaned against the brick planter that bordered the terrace.

She watched him with a vague hunger to be closer, but she didn't know whether it was a physical yearning or a need to have an ally in this uncharted territory of solitude.

"I still like you, Amanda." His voice called her nearer and she instantly obeyed. "I feel a little guilty admitting that. For some reason, I get the idea that we're supposed to glare at each other from opposite corners of the room."

"I know what you mean," Amanda said, relieved somehow that he was ill at ease with the situation too. "But I don't want to glare at you and they can't make me feel guilty about it."

"The omnipresent *they*." With a sly arch of his brow he turned his gaze to her. "Do you think 'they' are out to get us, Amanda?"

"Yes," she whispered with a solemn nod. "It's a plot to fix us up with blind dates."

"A fate worse than Chinese torture," he agreed gravely. "Do you think we stand a chance of escape?"

"Well, I intend to develop a burning interest in black cats, the number thirteen, and assorted other superstitions." She smiled at his puzzled expression. "Don't ask. Just keep it in mind in case Terri Henderson ever invites you to meet her sister."

"Cousin," Dain corrected. "She doesn't have a sister."

Amanda had difficulty controlling the surprised tilt of her lips. "You mean she's already—"

"Tried to fix me up?" He rubbed his chin in an oddly embarrassed gesture. "Yes, and I'm afraid I wasn't very polite in refusing either. Come to think of it, Terri has been sort of cool toward me since then." His eyes brightened with a tinge of devilry. "I told her I couldn't meet her cousin because I had to stay home and finish reading a particularly boring book."

"Dain!" Amanda released his name on an amused breath, glad, very glad, that he had ungraciously declined Terri's invitation. It was such a small, insignificant thing to please her so, but she couldn't deny that it did. And she couldn't deny the longing to reach out to him, but she made her fingers reach out to touch a leaf in the planter box instead. "What was the title of the book?" she asked.

"*How to Build Birdhouses for Fun and Profit.*" His hand closed over hers and stilled her fidgety movements. "Did you think I would lie just to get out of a blind date?" The amusement faded from his voice as with his other hand he cupped her chin and pulled her gaze back to him. His eyes, serious and searching, questioned her. "What are we doing, Amanda? Tell me what in the hell we're doing?"

She didn't pretend to misunderstand. "We're making the best of a difficult situation, Dain. It's hard to adjust to the idea of . . . divorce. Terri and Meg and Jerry—well, they're just trying to help."

"But no one can help, Amanda. No one except you, and that's the irony of it. I like being with you. I want to be with you, but I'm not supposed to want that anymore. We've been to dozens of parties together and, all of a sudden, I'm supposed to pretend I like coming alone?"

"I understand how you feel." She knew it was inadequate and trite, but he had caught her unprepared and she didn't know how to respond. "I—I feel the same way, Dain."

"Do you? Do you really, Amanda?" The pressure on her chin increased with the intensity of his voice. "I don't believe you understand anything at all."

Staring into the shadowy demands of his dark eyes, doubt swelled in her chest and she thought he might be right. What did she understand? How did she feel? *Really?*

"I understand loneliness," she said slowly, trying to find an answer for him and for herself. "And I feel out of place here. I'd like to pretend that nothing has changed, that

117

you and I are the same couple who used to belong with this group of people, Dain, but I can't. I don't even understand why I want to."

The brush of his knuckles along her cheek was a rough velvet caress, and he encouraged her to say more by the soothing stroke of his fingers in her hair. Amanda recognized the need to talk and a part of her wanted to share her thoughts, her feelings, with him, but she was reluctant to lower the walls of defense.

The closeness she felt could be an illusion manufactured by the events of the evening and the misleading softness of the moonlight. And even if it were real, what would it accomplish? She could tell him everything that was in her heart at this moment and it still wouldn't change the past. No words would ever take away the empty emotion she had locked inside her, the grief that Dain could never share. That, at least, she did understand, even if he didn't.

His uneven sigh held traces of impatience and resignation as he placed his hand at her nape and pressed her head against his shoulder. "Stop fighting me, Amanda," he murmured half to himself, and she wondered if he realized he had breathed the words aloud.

Her body complied with his request and relaxed into his warmth. She didn't want to fight him. Maybe it would be easier for both of them if she could, but she lacked the ability to direct any bitterness or anger toward Dain. He was still too much a part of her for that.

"We can't go back." Amanda whispered the warning to remind herself of the reality that existed outside his embrace. "We can't change what's happened."

Dain tightened his hold on her and then drew away to look down at her. "I just want to be with you now, Amanda. Is that too much to ask?"

It was, but she knew she was about to tell him it wasn't. Closing her eyes, she willed a lightness back to her voice and a smile to her lips. "What would you say to a walk along Baltimore's inner harbor and then, maybe, an early breakfast someplace downtown?"

The shadows were slow to leave his eyes, but at last Amanda saw the dawn of a smile. "Well, I intended to go home and read something dull, but if you'll buy my break-fast . . ."

"Did I say that?" Amanda feigned a frown and thought that now was the time to step out of his arms. But she didn't. "This is strictly dutch treat, Dain, take it or leave it."

His hands clasped at her hips and pulled her closer, stealing her opportunity to step away from him. "Would I be pushing my luck if I kissed you, Amanda? No, don't answer that, because it won't make any difference."

Her breath fluttered wildly in her throat and her gaze dropped compulsively to his mouth. This was asking too much, she decided firmly, and yet her lips parted with anticipation, waiting like a thirsty flower for a morning rain.

But he seemed in no hurry to erase the distance that separated them. Instead, his eyes lingered on her face, their message bringing a soft heat to her cheeks. Amanda wondered at the blush, wondered why she stood shy and acquiescent in his arms, wondered, too, why she had run madly from the mere mention of a blind date only to walk willingly into this far more threatening situation.

She was insane to allow this and insane not to allow it. The hummingbird rhythm of her heartbeat made a paradox of her thoughts. And then her breathing, her heart, her rational thoughts, stopped at the zephyr-soft meeting of their lips. It was a gentle kiss, reminiscent of other September nights under a sea of stars, and it graced her mouth for a moment as transient as the memory.

When Dain raised his head and released her, Amanda knew she was well and truly captured. Had he kissed her with passion or demanded a response, she knew she would have withdrawn at once. But he'd entrapped her with her own longing to be with someone who understood how very alone she had been tonight . . . until he had come to her rescue. Dain. She clung to his name and all the things it represented as she pushed aside any lingering doubts.

With a self-conscious movement she brushed at her hair and liberated a shaky laugh from her throat. "Do we make our escape one at a time?"

"No, too risky," he answered in a slightly husky voice. "I'm a little suspicious of 'them,' you know. We've been out here for quite a while. No telling what plans they've made in our absence."

Amanda's eyes widened with the sudden realization that she and Dain were probably accountable for at least a portion of the conversational hum inside the room. "What do you suppose they're saying?"

"Nothing of any consequence." He shrugged with deliberate nonchalance. "Besides, whatever it is will pale in comparison to what they'll think when we walk out the door together."

A tiny thrill ran through her at the word. Together. If only for a little while, she could be with Dain. To hell with what anyone might think. Her lips curved. "Lead the way," she commanded boldly and then added a hopeful thought. "You know, Dain, there's always a possibility that no one will notice."

His only answer was a slow grin as he took her hand and started for the door.

CHAPTER SEVEN

Anyone who had failed to notice the Maxwells' astonishingly serene departure was either blind, deaf, or had not been in earshot of Meg. At least that was what Jerry told Dain who, in turn, repeated it to Amanda a few days later.

Meg, of course, had been more subtle when she'd phoned Amanda the day after the reception. "You left the party so early, Amanda, that I had to call and make sure you were feeling all right." Amanda had said she felt just fine, that on the whole she'd thought the evening a little on the dull side. Then she'd asked with pseudo-innocence if anything exciting had happened after she left.

Meg took that as an open invitation to demand, more to the point, what exciting things had happened to Amanda after she left. Amanda had tried to avoid an answer, but had finally given in to Meg's persistence. Yes, she and Dain had left the party together. Yes, they had spent the night together walking—yes, just walking along the inner harbor. Yes, they had talked about a lot of things. Yes, yes, yes. And no. No, nothing had changed. Nothing.

It was the truth and, yet, it wasn't. Amanda recognized that each time she said it, each time she thought it. It was a tiny, inconspicuous, and totally necessary lie. But still, it was a lie. Wasn't it?

Amanda juggled the opposing thoughts for a full month after the night in Baltimore. What she had told Meg was undeniably true. She and Dain had spent hours walking, talking about nothing in particular. They had eaten breakfast in a small, all-night restaurant and afterward they had walked to where her car was parked. They had said good night, laughed together, and then traded the good night for good morning. He had smiled, told her to be careful. She had smiled, said thank you, and had driven home in the first light of dawn—alone. It had been a pleasant evening. An evening she might have enjoyed with anyone. But that's what was a lie. She had enjoyed it with Dain. *Nothing had changed.* The truth. A lie.

Something had changed in the past month. She knew it when Dain phoned to tell her of the stir their departure from the reception had created. She knew it when he called again the next day to ask her—what? Whatever he'd called to ask was buried under an exchange of light, bantering conversation. She knew it when he appeared unexpectedly to check the nearby boat dock for needed repairs and, for some reason, ended up staying for lunch. She knew it on the day she discovered him waiting for her after work.

I just happened to be in town, he'd said. *How about dinner?* She had smiled, pretending to herself that it was a simple coincidence. *I'd like that,* she had answered, knowing her casual acceptance was deceiving neither of them.

She had made a wonderful try at reasoning away all the coincidences, the phone calls, the unlooked for but not unexpected meetings, the idea that she was the object of a subtle and strategic courtship. It was almost too easy to think of excuses—loneliness, force of habit, any port in a storm, a problem of adjustment. But slowly the truth, like a light diffused through a prism, shone clear and pierced the security of her logic.

Dain didn't want the divorce. It was in his eyes when he looked at her, in his voice when he spoke, in his silence that told her heart what she wouldn't hear. He wanted her back. Amanda knew it as well as she knew him. The knowledge filled her with a kaleidoscope of frightening emotions and trembling possibilities. What did she want? And what could she realistically hope to have? Nothing had changed. That was the truth that evaded her, the lie that wouldn't fit into her careful rationale.

She had been positive when she left Dain that she had chosen the only possible course of action. She had been certain that he, too, wanted to end the nightmare their marriage had become. And she had been sure, deadly sure, that he no longer loved her. And now it seemed she had been wrong.

Amanda resisted the idea. She had chosen to do what she perceived as being right and the decision had cost her dearly. It was impossible to simply accept that she had been wrong. And yet the evidence was there in the tilt of his smile.

The divorce hearing was still pending, but postponed by a dozen delays. First there had been a delay of several weeks while waivers and interrogatories were filed and answered. It had taken even more time to receive the inventory list from Dain. Then the court date had to be postponed once and then again because Jerry had other legal commitments.

Amanda wondered if the seemingly trivial delays had been devised by Jerry at Dain's request. It seemed increasingly possible. Dain was slowly, deliberately, maneuvering her toward reconciliation. She was aware of it and made no move to stop him. Torn by the conflict of what had once been and what now was, Amanda didn't know what to do.

She couldn't go back. Too many hurts lay behind them. She was afraid to go forward. Too many uncertainties lay ahead. And still, she could not bring herself to say the words that would put a final and unalterable period to her past. Nothing had changed and yet, one small *maybe*—however cramped for space—took root in her heart.

It grew into a fledgling hope on the day Dain persuaded her to come sailing with him. It was a perfect day of crimson gold in a world of blue; the weather was crisp with the nip of approaching winter. They anchored in a small cove and ate their picnic in the late afternoon sunlight.

Relaxing on deck, Amanda savored the feel of autumn and the murmur of lapping water. The boat swayed, settled, swayed again, bringing a contented curve to lips that had known little else all day. A beautiful, perfect, unforgettable day. Her arms stretched up and up, pulling her Windbreaker taut across her breasts. Her head tilted back to face the sky. A bank of clouds scalloped the setting sun, jockeying for position along the horizon. It would storm tonight, Amanda thought, and sniffed the air for a promise of rain.

A dozen scents were carried on the breeze, but if rain was one of them, she didn't recognize it. How could she, when she inhaled the lazily sensuous fragrance that was so intricately Dain? Slowly her eyes sought him. Slowly her arms lowered. Helplessly she loved him across the red-checked distance of the tablecloth between them.

He was stretched full-length on the deck, hands behind his head, eyes closed, lips barely parted. His chest rose and fell with deep precision beneath the loose contours of his Windbreaker. His penchant for bare chest and cutoffs had given way to the October chill that necessitated jeans and a light jacket.

She watched him for a long time, absorbing the comfortable quiet between them. It was nice to feel so at ease, so at peace with herself and with him. Dain had been a wonderful companion all day, and pleasant memories of other sails across the bay surrounded her with familiar feelings. It was easy, here on the boat where they had loved so many times, to forget the boundaries that fate had drawn. She knew she shouldn't forget and yet, she wanted very much to remember the way she had felt about him then.

I love you. The words were a thick, pulsing ache inside her. So many memories were wrapped in those simple words. How many times had she said them? Amanda wondered. Fifty? A thousand times fifty? How easily they had once tumbled from her tongue. *I love you.* She had whispered them to him in the still of night, called them above the wind, teased him with them, drowned in the sweet mystery of saying them. *I love you. I love you.* Would she ever feel free to say them again?

Amanda tugged at the comb that held her hair. Deftly she pulled it loose and felt the slight breeze catch and tangle in the dark shoulder-length strands. She wished her hair were long enough to blow across her face and veil the image of the hard, male body that, even at rest, seduced her thoughts.

It had been a very long time since she had made love with him. Why did she feel this traitorous desire now? Now, when to touch him in even the most innocent way would demand questions, explanations, emotions that she wasn't ready to handle. Perhaps she would never be ready.

The thought closed around her like a damp morning fog, bringing with it a misty pain. Her gaze pulled away from him, went to the clouded sky, moved relentlessly back to his still form. A year ago . . .

The memory came swiftly, like a warning flash of lightning before the sharp clap of thunder. No. Oh, God, no. She didn't want to remember. . . .

"It's going to rain," she said with quiet panic.

The lazy arch of his brow said he wasn't asleep.

"Did you hear me?" The memory was coming stronger and she willed him to say something, anything, to deflect it. "It might storm, Dain."

He opened one eye, squinted upward for a second, then closed it again. "It might."

Frowning, Amanda put a hand to her cheek, felt herself tremble and let the hand fall to her lap. "Maybe we should get back. I'll just gather up the remnants of our picnic and the—the tablecloth and . . ." She struggled to think as her fingers groped for the cloth. It bunched in her grasp, spilling a can of pop. A dark stain pooled and she watched it spread, seeing instead a glimpse of hospital white and the gleaming metal of the incubator. She could hear the muffled blip of the monitor and the hushed whispers of strangers.

Dain, oh, Dain.

Her voice called his name in the distant realm of memory. Oh, God. She was going to remember. It was too late to stop the images that were already grating against her composure like sandpaper to glass. But Dain mustn't know; she couldn't let him see.

"I'll just take this below." How calm she sounded, how untroubled. She reached again for the cloth.

"Amanda?"

Her hand hovered, her throat closed. She shut her eyes and then forced them open to meet his. Richly brown and shatteringly perceptive, his gaze held her.

"What's wrong?" he asked, his tone probing, seeking to understand. He sat upright slowly and Amanda thought he moved as carefully as if he were skirting quicksand.

In self-defense she smiled . . . and knew that Dain wasn't fooled. Unable to utter even the smallest reassurance, she shook her head and kept her lips pasted in place. Inside she was crumbling, wanting to reach out to him, wanting to believe he could understand.

"Tell me, Amanda." It was softly commanding, almost a plea. His eyes wouldn't let her look away. "Tell me."

She couldn't. It had been a year. How could she tell him now what she hadn't been able to tell him then? How could she expose a grief that no one else could share?

I love you, Dain. The silent words filled her, mocked her with the incongruity of her emotions. She had been wrong to think that the loving would ever stop. Wrong, not to have made him understand the depth of her pain a year ago. Was it too late? Could he ever understand that sometimes loving just wasn't enough?

Tell me, Amanda. Tell me. Tell me. Like some strange litany, the words kept pace with his heartbeat and Dain

128

concentrated all his will power on her. She was so still that he had to curl his hands into fists to keep from grabbing her by the shoulders and shaking some life into her. He saw the resistance in the sapphire smoke of her eyes but on the sheer strength of his love for her, he compelled her to speak. Tell me, Amanda. Tell me you hate me. Tell me you'll never forgive me. No matter what you feel, tell me. Give me a chance to reach you.

She moistened her lips and he felt the tension flooding his lungs. It was like standing on a precipice, knowing he was going to fall, but daring to hope for rescue. *Tell me, Amanda.*

She had to tell him. The knowledge swept through her suddenly as if it had been waiting for an opportunity. He might not understand, but she had to try. Slowly, painfully, she forced the memory to become words and somehow she found the ability to voice them.

"I always thought you'd . . . I wanted you to be with me when our—our son was born." A shadow darkened his eyes and Amanda's stomach twisted with the reluctance to say anything else. Only the force of his gaze made her continue. "I don't blame you, Dain. I . . . really, I don't. I know how important the Reichmann account was to you. I know you had to go overseas. You couldn't have known the labor would start so soon. No one knew he would come so . . . so early. It's just . . ." She faltered, not knowing how to explain that she had needed Dain so badly then and how, in the frightening, expectant moments before birth, she had hated him for not being there. It wasn't fair. None of it was fair.

Amanda swallowed hard and closed her eyes against the swell of emotion. "He—he was so tiny, Dain. So little and I—I never even held him in my arms."

The agony of that denial slipped from her to weigh heavy on the evening air. Water lapped against the boat, whispering the regret over and over again.

"I know," Dain said in a raw, thick voice she didn't recognize. "I know, Amanda. Neither did I."

She felt the desolation of his words soak into her like a drop of water on a piece of cotton, and something within her rose to meet it. With a cautious, half-formed hope, her lashes slid upward and she studied him as he stared fixedly across the bay. Had Dain really wanted to hold their son? Had he felt the same impotent rage that she had felt during the hours of silent vigil outside the closed nursery door?

"Did you . . . ?" Amanda lifted a shaky hand to push back her hair from her forehead. She exhaled with difficulty. "Did you love him?"

Dain stiffened instantly, as if she'd struck him, and his gaze shifted to bore into her heart. For interminable seconds he sat immobile. Then one large and graceful hand spanned his jaw and rubbed downward to his chin. The fathomless darkness of his eyes centered on her and then turned away.

"How can you even ask me that?" His fingers moved to his forehead and pressed deep furrows there. "Yes, Amanda. Yes, I loved him."

A faint shadow of the approaching storm passed between them. She bent her head, seeking comfort in the words, but finding none. It wasn't what she'd meant to ask. She'd never doubted that Dain cared about their child, loved him in the tradition of all new fathers. What she had wanted to know was harder to put into words—things like how he had felt when he stood staring at his son through layers of windows and sterile air. Had Dain cried inside, as she had? Had he felt a part of himself draining away with each beep of the monitor? Had he made himself take long, steady breaths, believing that somehow it would help the baby to breathe?

Amanda traced a fingertip along the lifeline that curved across her palm. "Philip Christopher," she murmured the name, feeling now a sense of release mingled with the sadness. "He was very much like you, Dain."

Lifting her gaze, she saw Dain's fingers curl slowly into a fist, sending a ripple of tension through his muscled arms. In her mind's eye she saw a miniature hand that even in infancy bore the graceful imprint of Dain's paternity. Oh, God, she didn't want to think of this; she didn't want to see her son in the mature features of his father. What she wanted to see—what she would never see, not even for a single moment—was a look of pride and wonder on Dain's face as he held their baby, the symbol of their love, the fruition of their promise.

Amanda sighed with the distant rumble of thunder. She wanted the impossible; she wanted to change what had already been; she wanted Dain again, as if nothing had ever happened.

With a short, barely audible sound Dain turned toward her and caught her in the desperate look deep in his eyes. Amanda held her breath, wishing with all her heart that he could magically change the impossible into the possible.

"Amanda, I . . ." His mouth struggled with the words just as his need to comfort her struggled to penetrate the stone walls of her calm. "We don't need a baby to be happy. Many couples choose not to have children at all. Amanda, I don't need a child in order to have a satisfying life. I only need you."

Her reaction was sluggish and chillingly final. As the fragile trace of emotion in her eyes faded behind a cool façade, he knew she had misinterpreted his attempt at reassurance. In the space of a dozen heartbeats he watched her delicate features harden and he felt the distance that settled between them like an uninvited guest. The curve of her lips was a shield against emotion, against him, against anything that might hurt her.

"You need me to clean up this mess," she said in a falsely bright tone. Levering to her feet, she gathered the corners of the red checked cloth and pulled everything into a tidy bundle. His hand automatically reached for her and closed around her wrist, stopping her movements.

"Listen to me," he commanded hoarsely. "Tell me what I said to make you—" The question clogged together in his throat and he clamped a hold on his voice. "I didn't mean for you to—"

"I know, Dain. It's all right." The words were as meaningless as her hollow smile, and emptiness coiled inside him.

For several long seconds Amanda stayed quite still, held by the agonizing questions in his eyes. But when he released her wrist, she straightened and carried the picnic cloth belowdecks.

In the galley she braced her arms on the tiny cooking counter. A shudder escaped her control and jolted its way down her spine. Anger, guilt, grief, and regret whirled inseparably through her frenzied thoughts, accompanied by the staccato rhythm of Dain's words. *I don't need a child.* How could he be so insensitive? How could she have allowed him the opportunity to hurt her again? To remind her that he hadn't wanted the baby in the first place?

Amanda shut her ears to the sound of his footsteps

pacing the deck and she shut her eyes against his image. But he was there, in her mind. His face blurred with memory and then sharpened to crystal clarity. She pressed her hands harder against the galley shelf, willing herself not to see, not to remember. Dain had looked old that night and she recalled thinking that she should make him sit down. But she hadn't. His coat had been spotted with raindrops and she had thought that he should take it off and let it dry. But he hadn't.

Frowning, Amanda forced her lashes up and wondered why she recalled thinking such an odd thing. It hadn't rained that day. Her baby had died on a clear October afternoon. She wouldn't have left the hospital if it had been cloudy outside. Dain could never have persuaded her to go home and rest if the sun hadn't been shining with life-sustaining warmth. But the sun had fooled her and Dain had cheated her of the last few hours of her son's fragile life.

Her legs trembled as she walked across the cabin. She slumped onto the built-in berth and cradled her head in her hands. It hadn't been fair to blame Dain. He had only been concerned for her health. She knew that now. Three weeks of waiting, of fluctuating hopes and desperate fears had taken whatever strength she had left after the pregnancy. Dain hadn't even wanted her to be released from the hospital, but she'd rationally insisted that there was no point in paying for a room she no longer needed.

She remembered being very rational during those long days and nights in the hospital waiting room. Everything had been simple for her because nothing existed beyond the incubator that held her son. Dain hadn't understood that being close to the baby wasn't a matter of choice for her—it was necessary to her own existence.

There had been so many things Dain hadn't understood and therefore couldn't share with her. How did he remember the day their baby died? she wondered. Did he remember insisting that she let Meg take her home—just for a few hours? Did he remember the things she'd said? Did he remember that it hadn't rained? Amanda sighed in surrender and the memory seared through her mind with blinding accuracy.

Once home, she had fallen into a deep, exhausted sleep on the couch and, by rights, nothing should have disturbed her, but she'd heard the soft click of a key in the lock. The startled pounding of her heart had jerked her awake and for a few seconds she hadn't been aware of anything else. But like a butterfly emerging from a cocoon, the truth had stirred inside her. Dain was home and that could mean only one thing. . . .

Slowly she had swung her feet to the floor, stood, and turned to see him. His face was pale and drawn, his well-defined features shadowed, his shoulders held straight by some invisible thread of control. Silent, they faced each other across the width of a room that seemed to tilt and spin crazily in another dimension.

"Amanda." Dain said her name as if it were the only word he knew.

No! The denial tore through her with the force of a thousand screams, but left her lips in an agonized whisper. "No."

Her body sagged with the weight of loss and then her mind simply clicked off the unbearable emotion, separated her from the pain and focused on releasing the tension. "You shouldn't have left him, Dain. He'll be all alone."

Deeply etched lines made curious shadows in Dain's

face as he lifted his hand to her. "Don't, Amanda. It's over. He's gone."

"No," she stated. "He needs me. I should never have left him. You shouldn't have made me leave him, Dain. If you hadn't made me leave him—"

"Don't!" Dark eyes flashed with futile anger and then instantly softened with regret. "Oh, God, Amanda, please, don't."

She had glanced sightlessly around the room, thinking that she must get to the hospital, but she couldn't go barefoot. A panicky laugh rose in her chest and strangled in her throat. No, she couldn't go without her shoes. "I can't find them," she said, searching the carpet at her feet for a clue. "Hospitals have rules and I have to have my shoes. Help me find them, Dain. I've got to hurry."

He took a step toward her and stopped. "You don't need shoes. You're not going to the hospital."

Bewildered, she focused on him. "I have to, Dain. My baby needs me. He—"

"He died, Amanda. Our baby died." Dain moved to her side, his gaze never once leaving hers. When he raised his hand as if to stroke her cheek, she shrank from his touch and leveled a burning stare on him.

"But I have to see him." In some mysteriously maternal corner of her mind she had known that Philip Christopher wouldn't live and yet she'd never actually thought he could die. Her chin rose to challenge the truth. "Can't you understand, Dain? I have to see him."

"It's too late." His hand made another movement toward her and then abruptly dropped back to his side. "The arrangements are made, Amanda. You can't go to the hospital tonight. There's no point."

The harsh truth stained her heart with reality and her

gaze fell from his. Dain had made "arrangements" for her baby and had denied her a tangible part of acceptance. She didn't think she could ever forgive him that.

"It's your fault, Dain."

The memory suddenly frayed into dozens of disjointed segments and Amanda lay back on the berth. Had she really made such an awful accusation? Distractedly, she rubbed her temples, then let her hand rest at the base of her throat. She couldn't remember all that she'd said to Dain then, but she knew the ugly words had hurt as surely as she knew how helpless she'd been to stop their flow from her lips.

Without even trying, though, she could remember him shaking her in anger. His hands, rough and bruising, had gripped her shoulders. His eyes, glazed with a hidden agony, had stared into her very soul.

"Damn you, Amanda!" He'd almost yelled the curse at her. "Don't say that to me. Don't ever say that again." He shook her as if he could somehow erase the guilt that hovered mercilessly in the air.

When her body had stopped moving limply in his grasp, Amanda had let her head fall forward, shielding her grief behind the satin spill of her dusky hair. How could she have blamed him? It wasn't his fault. It was hers.

Lifting her head, Amanda had sought for words of apology, for words to make Dain understand, but came up empty. Her heart was too full of nameless pain. Thoughts, images, all had blurred before her eyes and she'd wanted only to lie down somewhere and sleep for a hundred years. "It should have been me, Dain." The admission had come involuntarily as she looked up at him and wondered if he could ever forgive her. "I should have been there. He needed me, don't you see? I should have died too."

The grip on her shoulders slackened and fell away. Dain walked to the fireplace and flattened his hands against the rock. Amanda had watched as if she were miles away, then she'd turned and left the room. Without really knowing how she got there, she'd opened the door of the guest bedroom and gone inside. She'd lowered her heavy body onto the bed and cradled one of the pillows in her arms. And there, in the unfamiliar room, in the dark, hidden from Dain and the world, she had closed the grief inside her heart and, finally, slept.

CHAPTER EIGHT

Dain stopped his frenetic pacing and stared at the approaching storm. Gray clouds tumbled over one another like naughty children vying for attention. The patches of blue sky overhead were deepening to twilight and the scent of rain was heavy in the air.

Clenching his hands in the pockets of his jacket, Dain faced the wind, feeling it toss his hair in the same way Amanda had tossed his emotions. He had come so close to reaching her—no, damn it! He had reached her. For a few minutes she had actually talked to him. She had wanted to tell him how she felt. And then he had said . . .

What had he said to send her retreating behind that mask of composure? He'd meant only to reassure her, to let her know that his concern for her well-being went deeper than his desire to have a child. She surely couldn't believe he would want her to go through that nightmare again. Hell, he didn't know what she believed anymore. Maybe she still blamed him.

The thought brought a wave of guilt and Dain clamped onto his self-control. He would not let her do that to him again. It hadn't been his fault. It hadn't been anyone's fault. Amanda hadn't meant to say those things to him that night. She hadn't even realized what she was saying.

Dain shifted his rigid stance, stiffening his resistance to the increasingly chill wind and balancing himself against the movements of the boat. It hadn't been words spoken that separated them—then or now. It was the unspoken feelings, the comfort of shared emotion that she had denied them both. How had he ever allowed her to drift so far from him? If only . . .

The hollow wish resounded with emptiness and flooded his mind with memories. If only he'd been more understanding of Amanda's longing to have a child, but he'd grown impatient with the endless frustration and the systematic lovemaking. When, at last, she became pregnant, he had breathed a sigh of relief that their life could get back to normal.

The relief had been short-lived though. Amanda had been uncomfortable and moody during the months of the pregnancy and he'd taken the easy way out. Work had proved a convenient ally, and he'd told himself that she was happier when he wasn't underfoot. If only the Reichmann account hadn't come along then. . . .

With a helpless frown Dain let the memory and the accompanying guilt return. He shouldn't have left Amanda, no matter how important the international hotel chain was to his career. She had said she'd be fine, the baby wasn't due for several weeks. She had told him to go and he had gone. The call had come only days after he'd arrived in Europe and he knew he'd never forget the nauseating fear that had engulfed him. Amanda needed him and he had juggled airline schedules to reach her as quickly as possible.

But Amanda hadn't needed him at all. He'd expected tears, hysterics, the same desperate worry that consumed him, anything except the calm, composed woman he found. She had been a stranger, someone he knew and yet had never seen before. She made no response to his attempts at comfort; she didn't seem to even realize he was there.

He had waited, knowing that time would help her cope with all that had happened. The days and nights became an endless wait, punctuated by fear. He hated the waiting and he hated the intricate wires and tubes that connected cold, impersonal machines to his infant son. He hated the look on Amanda's face as she stared through the nursery window, and most of all, he hated his own helplessness.

Then it was over and he'd realized the pain of waiting had been only the beginning.

Lightning streaked through the overcast sky and Dain focused on the momentary escape from the past. But, relentlessly, his mind continued to replay scenes from that late October day and eventually he stopped resisting.

He'd insisted that Amanda go home that day. Meg had offered her assistance and her own opinion that Amanda simply had to rest before she collapsed in exhaustion. If he'd known how quickly, how unexpectedly, a tiny life could end, he wouldn't have forced her to leave. But he hadn't known, and he hadn't known how much he would need Amanda in those final moments.

He'd never realized how much he depended on her quiet strength until then, and he'd never had any idea that being

140

a man could be so inadequate. He had talked to the doctor, made arrangements, even thanked the nurses for their concern and he'd done it all as if he were quite sane. But his desperate thoughts had been of Amanda, of his need to hold her and to be held by her. As he'd left the hospital, a part of him stayed behind and a part of him raced ahead.

He had no memory of driving home. The only thing that bound him to reality were the tears that splattered onto his jacket.

As he'd unlocked the door he remembered being grateful that at least Amanda had been able to rest for a while. She'd been awake, though, when he walked through the doorway—her midnight blue eyes had seemed enormously wide and her hair was tousled in long, dusky strands. Her slenderness and the ivory pallor of her skin gave an ethereal quality to her loveliness . . . a loveliness that even in his distress had wrapped itself in tranquilizing threads around his heart.

He was home. At last there was only himself and Amanda. No prying eyes to see that he wasn't the strong, capable man he pretended to be. Society's rules didn't apply here. He was home where he could close the door on the world and search for a grain of sense in the senseless reality of this nightmare. Amanda would hold him and cry with him. She would understand that just for a while he had to be a man who was weak with grief and frustrated with his own helplessness.

Home. Amanda. Inseparably entwined, but as he'd faced her in those first moments of agonizingly silent questions and answers, he'd thought he didn't have the strength to cross the room and find the warm comfort waiting for him in her arms.

In the next instant Dain had known how selfish his

thoughts were. Amanda needed his comfort more deeply than he needed hers. She had faced so much alone and somewhere, somehow, he would find the strength to help her as he'd been unable to help their son.

"Amanda." Her name dropped from his troubled thoughts because there didn't seem to be anything else to say. How should he tell her? What could he say? Was there any way to put the finality of death into words that consoled even as they stung?

"No."

Her whisper of pain shot through him like a knife, swiftly and keenly slicing into its target. He had thought his heart was too full to feel anything more, until the anguish in her eyes flooded him with compassion.

He had watched her pale, noticed the limp sagging of her body, and realized she was about to faint. But before he could think clearly enough to move toward her, something changed in her expression and he halted the movement unborn. A veil of denial fell misty and gossamer over her face to shield her from the reality.

"You shouldn't have left him," she had said evenly. "He'll be alone."

Bewildered sympathy welled inside him and he groped for something to say. His hand rose in a gesture of understanding. "Don't, Amanda. It's over. He's gone."

"No. I shouldn't have left him. You made me leave him, Dain. If you hadn't—"

"Don't!" The unfairness of her words and the confusing coolness of her voice jerked an angry response to the surface. He mastered it immediately, reminding himself that she was upset and her mind wasn't clear. He pleaded with her to understand. "Oh, God, Amanda, please, don't."

She had stared at him with the vacant expression of a lost child and then she had turned her head from side to side, her gaze seeking something beyond his comprehension. "I can't find them. Hospitals have rules and I have to have my shoes. Help me find them, Dain. I've got to hurry."

Fear wedged against the knot of emotion in his throat. What was she thinking of? Shoes? Hospital rules? Was it possible she hadn't understood? "You don't need shoes," he said as if he were soothing a child. He took a step toward her, but was stopped by a feeling of inadequacy. "You're not going to the hospital."

Her eyes had darkened in surprise. "But I have to, Dain. My baby. He needs me. He—"

"He died, Amanda." The truth rasped from his throat in a nauseating wave. "Our baby died." Dain wished he could pull the words back inside himself. He'd been too blunt. This wasn't the way he'd wanted to tell her. He was supposed to be holding her; he was supposed to be close to her, absorbing her sorrow and assuaging his own. His body obeyed the internal longing and he moved to her side. He lifted a hand to touch her cheek, but she shrank from him, bringing a whole new aspect to his pain.

"I have to see him." Amanda's voice shook with determination as she lifted her chin in challenge. "Can't you understand, Dain? I have to see him."

Dain had felt suddenly as if he'd stumbled into the wrong house. This wasn't Amanda, his wife, his lover, his friend. Amanda would never speak to him in such a coldly hostile tone. What did she want of him? He had done everything he knew to ease the situation, to make it possible for her to avoid the awful details of death. Again he lifted a hand toward her, but when he saw the withdrawal in her eyes he dropped it back to his side.

"It's too late," he told her in a voice both tired and defeated. "I've made the arrangements, Amanda. You can't go to the hospital. There's no point." He watched her assimilate the words and hoped for a sign that she understood, that she wanted the comfort he longed so to give.

"It's your fault, Dain."

He stiffened in horror at the thought, at the idea that she could ever think such a thing. It couldn't be true, could it? Had he failed to do something that he should have done? Had he done something to bring this tragedy into their lives? No, of course, he knew it wasn't true. Amanda was caught in the backlash of physical exhaustion and uncontrollable grief. Logically, he understood that, but still he felt the burden of guilt pressing into him.

Her voice went on, cataloging his sins, multiplying his own regrets. "You were supposed to be here when he was born, Dain, but you weren't. And you were supposed to stay at the hospital with him; you promised me you wouldn't leave him there alone. You never really wanted a baby in the first place, did you? I'll bet you're glad . . ."

He could stand it no longer. He had grabbed her shoulders and shook her until the black sheen of her hair whirled before his eyes.

Abruptly, Dain snapped off the memory and began to pace the deck once again. Why did he remember each and every word she'd said? Why hadn't time dimmed the scene in his mind? He rubbed the back of his neck and vowed that he wouldn't think further. He wouldn't remember her final words of betrayal. Everything else he could forgive. Everything except . . .

144

He could still see the cloud of raven hair as it had settled into disorder around her shoulders and face. And would he ever be able to forget the limp stillness of her body in his grasp or the remorse he'd felt at his own lack of control?

She had raised her head to look at him with nameless agony and he had wanted to soothe her, but he didn't know how to begin. For a long time she'd just stared at him, and yet, he'd known she wasn't really seeing him at all. She was focusing on some inner tragedy that shut him from her thoughts.

And then she had whispered the haunting betrayal of his love for her. "It should have been me, Dain. I should have died too."

Nothing in life had prepared him for such a moment. He had just lost his son, a tiny, minute part of himself that had left a gaping hole in the pattern of all he believed in. And now Amanda wanted to leave him too. He needed her, loved her with such quiet intensity that the thought of a world without her was inconceivable. And she wanted to die too. It was a betrayal of his trust in her, in his belief that she loved him . . . for better, for worse.

He'd let his hands slide uselessly from her shoulders, then he'd walked to the fireplace and braced himself against its solid strength. But it, too, felt cold and lifeless to his touch.

Dain couldn't remember how long he'd stood there, but he knew he'd finally realized that Amanda had left the room. Like a sleepwalker he'd followed her path, going without conscious direction to the guest bedroom. As he pushed open the door and saw her curled on the mattress, asleep, he'd known only that he wanted to take her in his arms and to feel her arms around him, protecting him from any further hurt. But he did no more than look at her before he closed the door and made his way to his own bedroom—the one Amanda had once shared. He'd sprawled across the bed and stared at the ceiling, aching with an uneasy knowledge that this was the beginning of long nights to be lived through—alone.

The wind caught the waters of the bay and slapped them playfully against the side of the boat. Dain shifted his balance with the movement and speared unsteady fingers through his hair. Solitude seemed to murmur around him with the coming night and, in the hazy twilight of memory, he could almost believe he heard the old gods of mythology laughing at his attempt to defy fate.

His gaze swung to the boat's cabin. There were no old gods, he thought bitterly, and there was no laughter in the wind. There was only Amanda. She was within the sound of his voice and still she couldn't hear him. He had tried to win her trust, to show her that a divorce was a mistake and he'd begun to believe that he was succeeding—until today. But at the first hint of raw emotion, she'd neatly bundled her feelings away and left him on the outside, alone.

The sailboat again swayed with the rhythm of the water and he moved automatically to check the anchor lines. The boat was secure, ready to weather the storm if it should intrude on the inlet where they were anchored. Dain let his gaze stray back to the door that led below-decks. Frustrated desires burned and flared into anger. He'd been on the outside for too long, and today would be the end of it. One way or another, Amanda was going to face him.

His deck shoes thudded hollowly on the shallow steps

and, once inside the cabin, it took a moment before his eyes focused on the dim outline of Amanda curled on the berth, asleep. It was too reminiscent of that other night, of the first time she'd shut him out so completely and his heart pounded erratically at the sight. *Damn her!* She wasn't going to sleep as if nothing had happened between them. He wouldn't allow her to escape so easily this time.

"Amanda." He spoke her name into a vacuum, enjoying the dull echo. She stirred and rolled onto her side, lifting a hand as if to push at the intruding sound.

"Dain?" Her voice was clear and free of the inflection of sleep, but he paid no attention.

"Get up, Amanda." It felt good to focus on his anger and it felt good to know that he was still capable of feeling an honest, unhesitating anger toward her. "Get up," he repeated. "We're going to talk."

She sat at the edge of the berth for a minute, eyeing him before she stood and clasped her hands behind her back. "I'm listening," she said quietly, as if she expected him to chat amiably about some mundane triviality.

Her composure only increased his frustration and he took a calculating step forward, watching to see her reaction. When none came he took another step and then another. "That's the trouble with you, Amanda. You say you're listening, but you never are."

She reached to snap on the light and he saw caution flicker in her eyes before she masked it. "I don't know what you're talking about, Dain. I'm listening to you now."

"Are you?" His gaze tackled her composure with determination. "And were you listening to me when you announced that we were getting a divorce? You never once asked if it was what I wanted. You never even asked for my opinion."

"But I knew—"

"How, Amanda? How in hell did you know? You stopped listening to me long before then. About the time you decided we should have a baby—"

"*We! We* decided, Dain." Her breasts rose and fell with her agitated breathing and then she turned her back to him. "I don't want to discuss this."

His hand closed over her arm and forced her to turn again. "Whether you want to or not, we're going to discuss this and anything else that comes to mind. You've shut me out long enough and I want some answers. Listen to me, Amanda, and listen well. I've given you time to think; I've played the game by your rules. You've had every opportunity to come to terms with your emotions. Now it's time to face the truth. I want you, Amanda. I have never wanted any woman but you. I do not now and never have wanted a divorce, and before we leave this place, you're going to tell me why you insist on getting one."

He saw the confusion in her eyes and watched it change to a distant uncertainty.

Her head bent slightly to guard her from his probing stare. "I thought—I *think* it's for the best."

"Best for you? Or me? Because they're not the same, Amanda. You can't arbitrarily decide something like that."

"You don't understand."

"You're right. I don't understand and I'll never be able to unless you're willing to talk to me."

Her lips formed a tight line of indecision and pain. "I tried, Dain. But I can't. I just can't."

The silence twisted inside him and he wondered what

to do next. She seemed to block him at every turn and his anger was subsiding in the face of her genuine distress. He swore softly and laid his palm against her cheek, keeping it there even when she would have moved away from his touch. "How can I get you to listen to me, Amanda, when I don't even know what I should say? Is there something I can apologize for? Something I can do to understand what has torn you from me?"

"No," she whispered. "Nothing."

His hand slid to cup her chin with a demanding pressure. "Then tell me what happened to us. Tell me why having a baby changed everything in our lives."

The veil of composure descended between them again and Dain fought the impulse to shake her now as he had done before. And in the same instant he recognized the tension that was building inside him. The feel of her skin against his palm was eroding rational arguments in favor of more tangible persuasion. His free hand moved un-prompted to her shoulder.

"There's no point in talking about this, Dain. You could never understand." Her breathiness registered in his mind and his eyes sought the gentle fullness of her lips.

"But I do understand this. . . ." His mouth found hers and he knew the die was cast. If Amanda wouldn't respond to his questions, perhaps her body would give him the answers. But as the sweet taste of her permeated his senses, Dain knew the reasons really didn't matter.

She was going to belong to him again . . . physically, if in no other way. She was going to remember what they'd shared and she was going to admit that some things never changed. Beyond that, he couldn't think and didn't care. His arms went around her, drawing her against him and ignoring her resistance, as if it weren't there.

Amanda felt her slight tension ebb with the insistent, rough satin texture of Dain's kiss. Of its own accord, her body melded to his, conforming to his symmetry like the last piece of a puzzle fitted into place to complete some predestined design. Her hands followed a once well-known path across his chest and over his shoulders. The nylon jacket was slippery beneath her fingers but couldn't conceal the vibrant warmth that she'd always found in his arms.

She was weak, logic insisted in a continuous repetition through her mind. Weak to allow herself these few stolen moments of forgetfulness. Weak to listen to the forbidden yearnings of her heart. But his lips—oh, the seductive feel of his lips—how could she fight such an enticement? Why would she even want to try?

His kisses clung to her mouth even when he lowered his head and breathed a sigh into the hollow of her shoulder. Dain held her close, his hands making small circles along her back. Amanda muffled the throaty whimper that almost escaped her so that Dain wouldn't recognize the sound of her desire, wouldn't know how much she wanted his lovemaking.

"Dain, don't do this to me." It was a protest of sorts, although her body flatly refused to move even a fraction away from his. Physically content to be in his embrace, she sent her thoughts spinning crazily in search of a viable argument. "It—it isn't right."

His soft, humorless laugh stirred the dark hair at her nape and feathered her neck with longing. "It feels right to me. In fact, this is the first thing that's felt right in a very long time." His arms tightened as he leaned back to look into her eyes. "And what's more, Amanda, it feels damned right to you too. Admit it."

Her eyelids closed, covering the truth of his words. But the evidence was there. Every part of her ached for him, and she knew Dain couldn't help but notice the rapid unevenness of her breathing and the hard thrust of her breasts against him. She hungered for him like a poet in search of a rhyme, but with the knowledge that easing the hunger could only complicate matters between them. Moving her hands to rest on his upper arms, Amanda pushed against him. "No, Dain. It isn't right and you can't really expect—"

"But I do expect it. You owe me this, Amanda. At the very least, you owe me this." His voice brought her eyes up to meet his as he enfolded her more securely in his embrace. "For months now I've tiptoed my way around your feelings, tried to consider how you felt, what you wanted, but tonight . . . tonight belongs to me."

Making a fleeting grab at her composure, she tried to ease out of his hold, but he held her fast without half-trying. Finally, with a low sigh, she stood still once again. "Why, Dain?"

"Because I want you and, at the moment, nothing else matters, not even how you might feel about it." He bent his head and captured her lips in a devastating challenge. Soft, sensuous, and evocative, the movement of his tongue against her own robbed her of the will to deny him—or herself.

He drew back and his gaze locked on hers. "But the nice thing is that you feel the same way, Amanda. You can make any excuse you like; tell yourself it's hard to break old habits or that the storm forced us to spend the night together, but in the morning I'll know and you'll know that neither of us had any other choice."

"There's always a choice," she said in a voice that was neither strong nor confident.

The tilt of his lips was leisurely, as was the light stroke of his fingers through her hair. Leisurely and mezmerizing. "Remember the first night we spent on the boat, Amanda? Our wedding night. You wore something black and deliciously wicked and I wore nothing at all. I held you for hours, wondering how someone as ordinary as me could be married to someone as extraordinary as you."

Amanda leaned against him and let her forehead rest on his chest. An illogical tear pushed at her lashes as she savored his confession, knowing that at the time it would have made her laugh, but now it tugged bittersweetly at her heart. Her wedding night, a memory separate and apart from so many other special nights with Dain. She had been shy and so incredibly happy that she'd felt almost guilty. And she'd lain in his arms, silently thankful that out of a world of choices he had somehow chosen her.

Idly, her fingers moved to the zipper pull of his jacket. Dain was right, she thought. Nothing mattered except the deep ache to hold him and touch him. But she was right too. There was a choice, the devil's choice, but still
. . .

Her hand slipped inside the nylon Windbreaker and nestled along the bend of his waist. Tingly pinpoints of anticipation flowed through her nerve-endings and quickened the rhythm of her breathing. She wanted to make love to Dain, she wanted to exhaust herself in his embrace and she wanted to drown in the sensations so long denied.

Curving her free hand around his neck and braiding her fingertips into his hair, Amanda lifted her head and met his eyes purposefully before she raised herself on tiptoe to reach his mouth. She kissed him lingeringly, moving against him with a control that surprised her. Heart pounding, desire pulsing madly through her veins, she separated their lips and then cradled his face in her palms for an endless moment before stepping out of his relaxed hold.

"Amanda?" His voice was thick as she took another step back and then another.

She stopped and arched one brow as she reached to unfasten the zipper closing of her jacket. The question in his eyes sharpened as he watched her shrug free of the lightweight coat, but the question vanished into dusky comprehension when she pulled the knit shirt she wore up and over her head. Her hair drifted into a provocative shadow about her shoulders as she bent to slip off first one shoe and then the other.

Amanda felt his gaze on her bare shoulders and on the lacy fabric that covered her breasts. Whispery thrills of pleasure skimmed down her spine and she trembled with the effort of maintaining a pretense at composure.

Dain. Dain. His name traced a path through her mind; a path that led straight to her heart as surely as her body would soon lead her into his arms. She unfastened her jeans, slipped them from her hips and pushed them to her ankles. Pulling one foot free, she kicked with her other foot and sent the denim skating across the floor.

A husky sound measured the silence and Amanda straightened, wondering if it had escaped his throat or her own? Her thumbs hooked under the elastic of her panties and the silk slid smoothly down her thighs and lay in a forlorn scrap at her feet.

His gaze followed, then made an unhurried retreat upward until it locked on the movement of her fingers at the front hook of her bra. Amanda held the flimsy covering

153

together, feeling her breath hover uselessly in her lungs and then, in the same instant, she released both breath and bra. The straps wandered down her shoulders and arms until the garment fell to the floor.

She stood, naked and vulnerable, allowing her courage to catch up to her actions. In the taut stillness of the cabin Amanda wanted to shiver with sudden nervousness, but Dain's steady, almost skeptical regard held the impulse in check. She had made her choice. She would give Dain all and more than he'd asked for, and in the process she would satiate her senses and finally be free of him.

Dain drank liberally of her beauty and dampened plaguing doubt with the stern admonition to leave him alone. He didn't want to know why Amanda had suddenly yielded. He didn't care. All he cared about was the determined craving of his body to possess hers.

But even as he caressed her with his eyes, he knew he cared. Her pliant acceptance could mean everything—or nothing. He was trapped by the myriad possibilities that faced him and his helplessness to choose any, save one. Amanda. The beginning and ending of his dreams.

Without a wasted motion he stripped the jacket from his shoulders and worked loose the buttons of his shirt. He watched her carefully as the material parted and he slipped it off. Her gaze settled on the wispy gold curls that clustered on his chest and he remembered how she had once told him that he had one hundred and thirty-one chest hairs because she had counted them while he slept. Just enough, she'd said, adding that one hundred and thirty-two would have been gaudy.

Silly thing to think of now, he thought as he kicked off his shoes and fumbled with the snap on his jeans. But at least the distracting memory kept his hands from shaking visibly. There were memories everywhere on the boat, but he felt uncomfortable with them. Reminiscing should be kept for another place and time. This rendezvous with Amanda was different because, for the first time, there was no solid commitment, no promise of forever. He couldn't count on having more than what she offered to him right now. And whatever happened, he intended to take all that she would give.

After what seemed an unconscionably long while, he stepped out of his jeans and briefs. He felt awkward standing before her, as if he were unaccustomed to her intimate gaze. It had just been too long, too damned long. Deliberately, he approached her, putting his hands on her shoulders and rubbing the length of her arm to wrap her small fingers in his palm.

Hesitancy blended with eagerness in her piquant face and Dain noticed the soft quiver of her lower lip. It pleased him to recognize the signs of her own uncertainty. He wanted to whisper love words, but whether to reassure her or himself he didn't know. And he sensed that Amanda would turn away from spoken promises. What happened between them now had to be silent and more irrevocable than evanescent words.

He walked backward to the berth, pulling her with him. Sitting on the edge, he drew her close and pressed his lips to the pulse at the base of her throat. His hands explored her, reacquainting himself with her shape. He found the tip of her breast hard and tantalizing to the rough circling of his tongue. Long-suppressed passions swelled and throbbed inside him and he increased the pressure of his massaging kiss.

With light strokes his fingertips moved over her skin, remembering the responsive places, lingering just long enough to tease and tune them to his private orchestration. The crescendoing melody faltered, though, as he ran his sensitive palms across her stomach. If he hadn't known her body so well, he might have missed the almost imperceptible changes in her. But he did know and he noticed the difference.

Amanda had always been slender, firmly curved, and perfectly formed. That hadn't changed—the difference seemed more in the feel of her. It was as if pregnancy had smoothed angles and mellowed the taut muscles of youth into full maturity.

Dain closed his eyes with the realization that brought a mixture of sadness and pride. He'd never had any intention of changing her and yet the simple fact of his love had done so. Did she regret the tiny marks that would always remind her that once she had carried the seed of his love? He laid his cheek against her breast as his hand moved over her stomach in tender tribute. Dear God, he thought, please don't let her regret something so beautiful.

Breathlessly, Amanda absorbed the scent and sight and feel of his nearness. Her fingers were buried in the tawny richness of his hair; her body was lost in the sweetness of his touch; her heart was a willing hostage to the magic that drugged the air with surrender.

Here, in his arms, she found a serenity she'd thought never to experience again and she wanted to savor it to the fullest. Whether it was right or wrong she no longer cared. For a little while, time would cushion the truth, fuse the past into the present and let her love Dain for one splendid moment.

He had claimed the night for his own, but it would belong to her too. Hours, moments, a lifetime—fugitive promises in a confusing tapestry, but she would have the memory of tonight—one silver thread to remember for always, no matter what.

When she felt him grow still, Amanda called a halt to the weavings of her mind. A reluctant shiver of awareness seeped through her as she realized the questing exploration of his hands had a new purpose. The marks of pregnancy were faint on her skin, but they were there nonetheless. And Dain had noticed.

Amanda closed her eyes tightly, wanting to hold on to the lovely feeling of belonging, but it slipped further and further away with each inquisitive brush of his fingers. Even now, when she'd almost managed to forget, he had reminded her, reminded her of the pain that lay between them like two parallel lines that stretched to infinity without ever once touching.

His stroking stopped and a low groan of sadness rumbled from his throat as he bent his head to kiss her stomach softly. Did he see her as scarred? Less than what she had once been? She attempted to block the thought from reaching her fragile emotions. Like the darkness blankets the night, she gathered her feelings about her for shelter. What he thought didn't matter. Nothing mattered, except taking and giving until there was nothing left.

Flames of need flicked at her reason and she placed her hands on his shoulders, pressing him down, down into the mattress. His eyes smoldered in surprise, but his arms went around her, drawing her with him.

She lowered herself until the searing heat of her flesh blended into his. A smile that wasn't quite a smile touched her lips and vanished, but Amanda felt its sting. Loving Dain had become a paradox, an emotion separate and apart from her. Even as she yielded herself to the beautiful sensations, she felt distanced from him and yet so close she could melt into his very being.

She was fire and ice, a cold December rain and a tropical summer storm. As her lips covered his in a pleading kiss, she moved feverishly to assuage the spasms of urgency that shuddered through her. Their bodies joined, but that wasn't enough for her. There would never be enough; she knew that with each tympanic beat of her heart. But still she made love to him desperately, as if she could rid herself of the yearning, as if somehow she could free herself of him.

Slowly, she recognized the calming caress of Dain's hands and just as slowly, she felt herself begin to respond. He gentled her, quieted her frenzied movements and murmured her name until it became a rhythmic part of her breathing.

For a long time he held her, his lips a constant reality in a world of dreamy sensation. Along her neck and into the soft hollows of her shoulders his kisses burned. He stroked her, letting his fingers graze her inner thigh and then letting them stray upward to brush against the swell of her breast. As the tantalizing teasing grew more serious, Amanda allowed herself to move again. Her body tightened with a ripple of excitement and the intimate delights of rediscovery.

Dain was as solidly male as she remembered. His skin was rough and smooth to the touch, like richly napped velvet. He tasted of salt spray and the clean scent of outdoors clung to him with enticing promise. His body was a muscular pillow that accepted her weight without protest and contoured to fit her very feminine outline.

The sailboat berth offered only moderate comfort, but Amanda knew she couldn't have wished for more than

Dain's warm embrace. It was like sinking into a feather bed and feeling it puff and billow until it formed a downy cradle. Dain enclosed her in the same cushiony way.

With consummate skill he created a pleasurable tension inside her. Her breasts were firm and heavy against the frictioning texture of his chest. She felt his passion build, knew the wondrous mystery of being a part with him in this ageless, but always new union. Rhythmically, she moved with him until her thoughts and yearnings meshed into his with perfect accord.

She heard the pelting tempo of rain outside and exulted in the elemental storm within her that whipped at long-denied passions and forced her to feel and react. With a lingering sigh that escaped her throat as a whispery plea, Amanda gave herself up to the tempest that was, and always had been, surrender.

As if he had been waiting for that sigh, Dain captured it and returned it to her lips. His breath filled her and his tongue curled around hers in an erotic symbol of their joining. With swift, steady tenderness he loved her until, at last, she lay drained but satisfied in his arms.

Even after his breathing was sleepily deep and regular, Amanda stayed nestled in the curve of his side. Her mind wandered through memories of other nights when she had known contentment with Dain. Could she dare to hope that the feeling would linger? Was there a chance that tonight marked the beginning of new dreams? Of a future together?

She wouldn't let her thoughts drift further into fantasy. At the moment everything was a muted blur; truth blended into wishes, and emotions merged with physical serenity. A good marriage depended on mutual understanding, and whether she and Dain could ever build that foundation again was an undecided question.

She had given herself to Dain tonight because she had wanted to resolve the conflict of heart and mind. But she had only proved that there was no resolution. Even in the midst of loving him, of being caught in the wild winds of her own passion, there had been a corner of her heart that remained her own—a closed door that would not open. And heaven alone knew if there was a key.

"Amanda?" From the silence his voice came, husky with unspoken promises. "Come home to me."

She couldn't stop the trembling that stripped her contentment in a matter of seconds. Oh, Dain, she thought, why did you have to ask now?

"Dain, I . . ." Her words trailed into emptiness. For him the answer was a clear-cut yes or no, but for her it was colored by varied shades of gray. She searched for the right way to say Maybe . . . Someday . . . but not now . . . not yet. She searched and Dain waited for the answer she could not give.

Slowly, she felt him shift on the narrow berth and then she shivered as he pulled his arm from around her. He reached up and snapped off the light, then lay back beside her. With the darkness, Amanda realized the small but significant space he'd placed between them.

They were two people who shared the same bed and the same empty longings—two people who had just shared a special expression of love and who now were as separate as it was possible for two people to be.

Tears welled in her eyes and evaporated with her guilty frustration. This was all her fault, from beginning to end. And yet, even knowing that, she felt powerless to bridge the chasm that existed between her heart and Dain's.

Powerless to prevent the good-bye that she was sure would come with the morning—a morning that was still hours away and yet would dawn all too soon.

CHAPTER NINE

The call from her attorney came two days after Dain had left her with a good-bye as frosty as the Chesapeake morning.

"Mrs. Maxwell, good news!" The gruff voice was professionally pleasant and to the point. "The final hearing for your divorce has been set."

"Oh," Amanda said, and then added with resignation, "I don't suppose there will be any more delays?"

"No need to worry about that. Mr. Maxwell's attorney assured me that his client wanted the final decree as soon as possible. Still, the court schedule was so full that six weeks was the best I could do. December twelfth, that's the date. You'll have your divorce in time for Christmas."

"Oh," Amanda repeated, her fingers automatically reaching for a pen to make a note of the appointment. Her mind skittered away from the date she scribbled on the cover of the telephone directory. December twelfth.

* * *

On the twelfth day of Christmas, my true love gave to me . . .

Amanda frowned at the scrap of nonsensical song and made herself concentrate on the voice at the other end of the line. But the conversation was already being concluded and she barely had time to say thank you before the phone connection was broken.

As she replaced the receiver in its cradle, her pen circled the date again and again. Amanda stared at the movements of her hand and the bold finality of what she had written. December twelfth—divorce. There was some mistake, she thought. You were supposed to get presents for Christmas, not a divorce.

. . . my true love gave to me . . .

The song wouldn't leave her alone and she walked to the window to look blankly out at a windy, gray day. Dain was giving her what he thought she wanted—only she knew it wasn't what she wanted at all. She wondered how he would react if she called him and told him that she'd made a mistake. What would he say if she asked him if she could come home?

Amanda lifted the weight of hair off her nape and then let it fall again onto the collar of her sweater. Oh, if only it could be that simple. If only she could believe that going back to him would solve everything. But how could she even consider the possibility when she knew that the relationship she offered would be less than what she'd given before?

Time could mend the separation of their hearts and

163

bring a modicum of normalcy to their lives, but it couldn't erase the scars. There would always be at least one barrier between herself and Dain, one subject that couldn't be discussed and one memory that would keep them from sharing the total, unreserved intimacy of marriage.

Maybe if she had loved him less, it wouldn't have seemed so important, but she did love him and it was important.

Absently, she ran her hands over the smooth fabric of the draperies. December twelfth. Six weeks away. The thought made her heart as heavy as the overcast sky and another fragment of song drifted to mind.

Until the twelfth of never, I'll still be loving you.
. . .

Amanda sighed as the first raindrop spattered against the windowpane. If only she could believe that loving would be enough. . . .

Snow began to fall early on Thanksgiving morning and, in guilty relief, Amanda canceled the planned visit to her parents' home. By late afternoon the sun was setting on a world of winter white and she'd stayed indoors as long as she could. She donned jeans, sweater, heavy socks, boots, down jacket, muffler, and stocking cap before stepping into the soft silence outside her door.

Amanda walked all the way to the boat dock and stood for a few minutes looking at the icy veneer that glazed the surface of the water. Turning to retrace her path, she was careful to match boot to bootprint so that only one set of prints disturbed the smooth, snow blanket. The childhood game brought a sudden smile as she remembered how Dain had teased her for playing it.

Dain. He was never far from her thoughts, but today he seemed especially near. Maybe it was just the holiday and the memory of other Thanksgivings spent with him, but Amanda felt the weight of his absence as if it were the coat that she wore. She wondered where he had gone for the holiday, whom he'd talked to, if he'd thought about her.

She stopped at the edge of the road and looked back to check her neat path. Her gaze settled on Dain, who stood several yards from her on the trail that led from Martha's house to the dock. Her lips curved in spontaneous greeting and she lifted a hand to catch his attention before the reason for his stillness trapped her in mid-movement. He hadn't wanted her to see him, and she realized with heart-tugging sadness that she wouldn't have—if she hadn't been playing the game.

But now that she knew he was close, Amanda couldn't just walk away. She had to talk to him, had to hear his voice. And maybe she would just mention, casually, that she really didn't want a divorce.

He was turning to leave and she called to stop him, but the sound was so low that he didn't hear. Her breath hung in her throat as she took a hurried step toward him and suddenly, she was running. "Dain," she called louder this time. "Dain, wait!"

He kept his back to her, but he stopped and waited for her to catch up to him. Amanda noticed the stiff way he held himself and she knew she should have pretended not to see him, but she'd missed him so. She raised her hand to touch him, then dropped it without so much as brushing his sleeve. "Dain?" It was a whisper that carried all her futile wishes, and when it brought his gaze around to her, she forgot everything except the dusky pain in his eyes. Oh, God, she'd never meant to hurt him.

"Hi," she said, just to break the emotion that bound them in silence. "Happy Thanksgiving."

His smile seemed to come from a great distance. "Happy Thanksgiving."

Her glance went past him to the trail beyond and then returned. "Have you been at Martha's all day?"

"Yes."

"I suppose you had a traditional Pemberton dinner?" Amanda's lips curved with memories.

"Believe it or not, we had turkey with all the trimmings." Dain's smile eased into a more natural tilt. "Mr. MacGregor told Martha that it was downright heathen to have lobster and devil's food cake on Thanksgiving. She fussed all through dinner and said she refused to be thankful for turkey."

Amanda laughed. "I'll bet it didn't affect her appetite, though, did it?"

"Not noticeably," he answered, the dark expression in his eyes lightening a little. "What about you? Did you have dinner with your parents?"

She adjusted the muffler at her neck and then pulled the stocking hat more firmly over her ears. "I was supposed to drive over this morning, but, well, with the snow and all, I decided to stay home."

"Alone? You should have come to Martha's."

The arch of her brow attempted a nonchalance she didn't feel. "I wasn't in the mood for company," she defended herself weakly.

His jaw clenched and then relaxed. "Oh, Amanda." He exhaled the words with a sigh and raked his fingers through his hair. "I'll bet you weren't in the mood for dinner either. Do you want to walk back to the house with me and have something to eat?"

She refused with a shake of her head. She would have liked to walk with Dain, but she definitely did not want to see either Martha or a turkey sandwich. "I was thinking that some hot cider and a cozy fire would be nice, but since I don't have a fireplace, I guess I'll just add a dash of something fiery to the cider. Would you—" The invitation dwindled to nothing as she saw him look away.

"I think I'd better refuse," he said quietly, and silence reigned supreme for the space of a deep breath. "The last time I accepted an invitation like that, I ended up soaking my feet in a pan of hot water for the better part of an hour."

Her gaze flew to meet his as the warm glow of memory filtered through her. He remembered that first Christmas together, she thought. And not only that, he remembered how silly in love she'd been. She had wanted to be so sophisticated, but they'd gone for a walk and she'd tripped and fallen in the snow. Dain had teased her unmercifully until she'd managed to push him off balance and topple him into the snow beside her. They'd wrestled and played until they were both cold and wet, but thoroughly heated by the kisses they exchanged. And later she'd insisted with proprietary concern that he drink a mug of cider and soak his feet to prevent a chill.

She couldn't restrain the upward slant of her lips. "And all this time I thought you liked playing footsies in my old aluminum dishpan."

The memory faded from his eyes and he jammed his hands into the pockets of his ski coat. "I did like it—at the time." His eyes kept straying from hers and then returning, as if he didn't want to look at her but couldn't bear

167

not to. "Besides, there's no danger of either of us taking a chill today, is there?"

Amanda felt colder than she had in a long time and she wanted more than anything to win just one warming smile from him. "I could always manage to trip and fall," she offered in a teasing voice that sounded oddly serious.

Dain hesitated and she noticed how unnaturally tense he seemed. "Amanda, I . . . maybe I'd better get back to Martha's. She and MacGregor may need a referee by now."

His excuse uprooted her frail composure as if it were a seedling in a strong wind, and she stared hard at the ground. Dain was uncomfortable with her and a wave of anger wound through her, anger at herself for forcing this meeting on him, for hurting him when it was the last thing she'd meant to do. She'd just wanted to be with him for a few minutes.

With a false smile of understanding she met his eyes. "It's getting late. I'd better start back myself before it's too dark to see my footprints. Remember how you used to tease—" The words choked in her throat and she couldn't pretend anymore. "I'm sorry, Dain," she whispered hoarsely. "I'm so sorry. I never wanted any of this to happen. Please, believe that. It's just that . . . I just didn't know how to stop it."

A bleak expression tightened his jaw and whitened the tiny scar at his eyebrow. Amanda spun away from him, unable to face his reaction, whatever it might be. With a murmured "good-bye" she started walking, her entire concentration on putting one foot in front of the other. When she heard him behind her, she kept on, wishing with every step that she had the courage to finish what she'd begun—the courage to stop running from him.

He was beside her then and the quiet twilight was fraught with questions. Amanda couldn't think of a single word to say. She just kept going as her mind searched for answers.

"All right, Amanda." Dain's voice was low, resigned, but infinitely tender. "Are you going to fall on your own initiative or do I have to trip you?"

It was the very last thing she'd expected, and she stopped short, seeking his gaze with her own. He stopped, too, and they stood for an eternity, just looking at each other. Tears stung her eyes and pulled her mouth into a shaky line. "Oh, Dain," she whispered. "How can you even stand to be near me?"

"I love you, Amanda." His hands cupped her shoulders and pressed hard into her soft jacket. "God help me. I love you."

Emotion clumped in her throat as he drew her into the shelter of his arms. She denied the yearning to simply rest on his strength and made herself lean back in his embrace. "Dain, I don't want the divorce. I can't go through with it. I thought it would be easier for you, for both of us, but I was wrong. I've been wrong about so many things and I . . . Please, I don't want a divorce."

He placed his fingers against her mouth as if he could capture her words and hold them in his hand. There was a bare tremor in his touch as his fingers moved along her cheek, pushed at the stocking cap and finally threaded into the ebony satin of her hair. Amanda shivered, wanting to say more, wanting to share all the thoughts and feelings that avalanched inside her. But where could she begin?

The world around them grew hushed with night and she longed to absorb the quiet into herself. She took a deep breath, released it, tried again. Her eyes locked with his in a moment that could have lasted a second . . . or a lifetime.

On a sigh Amanda grabbed a thought at random and gave it voice. "I believed you didn't love me and I wasn't even sure I still loved you. I had to leave. There didn't seem to be anything else I could do. Nothing was in perspective and I . . ." She faltered, groping for a way to make him understand. "I do love you, Dain. Even now, I'm not sure I've sorted everything out, but I know I love you. I know I want to make our marriage work. It has to work, because I don't think I can face any more of this emptiness."

"Amanda."

It was a question and an answer, just as the gentle blending of their lips was both bitter and sweet. When Dain lifted his head she ached to heal the pain that divided them. "Let me learn how to love you again," she said softly. "Stay with me."

The husky plea wove delicately through the evening air, drawing them together like the moon draws the tide to shore. In unspoken commitment Amanda's hand sought his and nestled there as they turned and walked toward her house. Dain seemed as reticent to break the silence as she, and Amanda wondered if he was feeling a measure of uncertainty too. Strange, that she should feel cautious of this impulsive truce that had been forged from her heart's wistful yearnings. The impulse had been born of love, and she couldn't regret one word she'd said to him. Somehow, some way, she would keep this promise. She would not fail him again.

She glanced at his profile and recognized the tiny doubts that feathered from the corners of his mouth. Dain, oh, Dain. Her heart closed around his name, sheltering him from her thoughts. He was everything that she was not—strong, determined, knowing what he wanted from life and what he could have, and he knew how to make them the same. Dain was a survivor, a fighter, and she had never learned to be either. Life had always been easy, giving her an abundance of family, friendships, and love with hardly any effort on her part.

But that was the past. It was time she learned that some things were worth fighting for, and her marriage was one of them. Nothing could ever be as it was, but she would make Dain happy. I will, she vowed to the obstinate memories that wouldn't release their hold on her heart.

As they reached the porch and mounted the stairs, Amanda squeezed his hand. "I love you, Dain."

He opened the door and smiled down at her upturned face. "I know."

Was there a distant sadness in the unreadable darkness of his eyes? No. She shut the idea from her mind and preceded him inside the house. From this moment on, Dain would not know sadness, not because of her.

Amanda pushed one hand against the entry wall to balance herself while she pulled off one boot, then the other. She placed the boots side by side, laid her socks on top, and took off her jacket and muffler, only then remembering that she had forgotten to retrieve her stocking cap from the snow. But one glance at Dain shedding his cold-weather clothing and looking so endearingly familiar and she forgot the cap again. He put his wet boots next to hers and pleasure rippled clear to her fingertips at the sight. It had been a long time since anything had looked so cozy or so right.

With a crooked smile he closed the door and Amanda slipped her arms around his neck. "What shall we do

171

first?" she asked with a saucy arch of her brow. "Would you prefer a mug of cider or would you rather soak your feet?"

"Hmmm." He pretended to consider while his hands found the slender indentation of her waist. "I think I'd prefer a soak in the bathtub—with you."

"How wonderfully decadent. From dishpan to bathtub in one easy lesson."

He tugged her closer. "A lot you know about it," he scoffed gently. "There's an art to soaking correctly, you know."

"Really?" Her eyes widened and she inched her lips nearer his. "I always liked art appreciation class and I am a quick study, you know."

His laughter was nice—not as effortless as she would have wished for, but nice although it died too quickly. "Amanda, Amanda. I've missed you even more than I thought possible. I should never have let you go in the first place, but I didn't know how to convince you to stay. Then that day on the boat when we talked about the baby—"

No, Dain, no! She pressed her fingers to his mouth, stilling the words. "Shhh," she murmured. "This is the time for loving, not talking." Substituting a kiss for the pressure of her fingers, she moved against him persuasively and felt the response grow within him. "I want to love you, Dain," she whispered huskily. "I want to lose—and find—myself in loving you. Please, plea—"

He smothered her almost desperate entreaty with lips that drank thirstily of her sweetness. Amanda quivered with the need to satisfy him, to give to him all that she could give and to be whole again. When he lifted her and carried her into the front room she clung to him as the sky clings to the sunset, unwilling to relinquish even one warming ray.

The plush fiber of the carpet cushioned her weight but chafed at the sweater she wore. She was glad that Dain wasted little time in removing it and her jeans. He seemed in no hurry to banish her silky underthings though; his lips nipped at the sheer fabric covering her breasts in deliciously stimulating play.

Amanda watched his face as he touched her and she felt incredibly, delicately feminine beneath the tender expression in his eyes. Dain was a tender lover. Always, from their first kiss, she had marveled at his gentleness and the care he took in pleasing her. He was skilled in building her desires to fit the design of his passion, and already she could feel the fire inside her simmering to life.

The slow, velvet seduction of his hands was ecstasy. Amanda closed her eyes as a shiver spiraled upward from the tips of her bare toes. Her body trembled with the demanding, yearning ache to know him, to touch him, to be a part with him in the intimacy of love.

She curled her leg over his and rubbed his denim-covered calf with her foot. The coarse fabric moved just a little and Amanda smiled as she made contact with his hair-rough skin.

Dain raised his head to look at her accusingly. "Your foot is cold."

"I know." She snuggled the foot farther inside the leg of his jeans. "But you're very warm." Her hands went to his shoulders, urging him down. "I think I might be much warmer if you took your clothes off."

"But then I might be cold." He bent to nuzzle the sensitive hollow below her ear.

She turned her head, seeking his earlobe with her

tongue. "Live dangerously," she breathed before arching her body persuasively against his.

An inarticulate murmur rumbled from his throat and ended as a caressing kiss. Her lips parted in acceptance and moved lightly beneath the soft contours of his mouth. Her arms curved around his neck; her palms cupped the muscular ridges of his shoulders. Spindrift sensations shimmered through her like rain in the moonlight.

With the ease of remembrance, his hand glided over her, lingering to stroke and tantalize the smooth pleasure points on her skin. Then, reluctantly, he drew back, letting his kiss cling momentarily before he released her lips and gazed down at her with smoldering umber eyes. "Is it my imagination," he asked huskily, "or is it getting unbearably warm in here?"

Amanda cradled his face in her palms and smiled. "Unbearable," she agreed as her fingers went to the button tab of his shirt. With impatient, but steady movements she unfastened the buttons and then tugged the material from the waist of his jeans. He lay still while she pulled the shirt up and over his chest. Pliantly, he shifted to aid in slipping it from his shoulders and head. She couldn't resist the appeal of his bronze chest and pressed a hungry kiss there.

Her hand went to his belt buckle, but he stopped her and drew her fingers to his lips, touching them one by one as his eyes held hers. Then, with a lithe, graceful motion, he stood and stripped off the rest of his clothes.

His tanned, virile body was as familiar as the response it evoked, and Amanda let her gaze admire him while the slumbrous desire awakened to fiery life. Her fingers touched his ankle and etched a feathery trail upward along his calf. Slowly, he sank to his knees and her palm smoothed his thigh with easy, unhesitating strokes. She

174

caressed him with her eyes and then with her hands, lovingly, gently, knowing and savoring the effect.

As she coaxed him down beside her she marveled at the perfect planning that had created male and female, Dain and herself. She was formed for his pleasure just as he was made to pleasure her. Individual differences bonded into an exquisite union of body and spirit.

Dain explored the silken curve of her stomach and the slender line of her inner thigh as he slipped her panties from her. He pulled the strap of her bra down her arm and freed one breast. Sensuously, his tongue circled the darkened tip while he unfastened the hook and lifted the bra away. Suddenly, Amanda was throbbing with the need to possess and to be possessed. Dain, her heart called, its rhythm staccato and quick against her ribs. Her back arched in fierce longing.

He answered her mute appeal with a stormy taking of her lips. When he lowered himself onto her, she welcomed him with the urgency of beautiful memories and the breathtaking splendor of reality. The moment of joining, the feel of flesh against flesh, arms and legs entwining in the glorious embrace of love—all of these, she experienced anew, remembering their magic and yet learning them as if for the first time.

His chest moved over her in chafing arousal, teasing her breasts into taut peaks of yearning. Her hands discovered the even slope of his waist and followed it to sinewy hips and muscled thighs that pressed erotically into hers. She moved as one with him, the burning sweetness of their loving filling her as nothing else could.

"I love you, Dain." The words floated through her and from her to linger like music in the air. And then she was gathered closer in his arms as passion fused them together like two colors that blended into one.

Dain lay awake long after Amanda had led the way upstairs to bed. She had curled as close to him as possible and gone to sleep.

He rested his head on his hand and gazed down at his wife. His, he thought with fierce possession. He had won her back. She was his again. He had won.

In the darkness his eyes caressed her, seeing more from memory than in actuality. She was the loveliest woman he had ever known. Her complexion was as creamy and smooth as a child's, her eyes, so deeply blue that the heavens paled in envy, were hidden by thick, heavy lashes as black as the strand of hair that graced her cheek. Reverently, he brushed the strand back and tucked it into the cloudy darkness that splayed across the pillow.

His heart ached with emotion. Amanda was all he asked of life. And she was here beside him just as he'd determined she would be. Yet, even in sleep, she'd moved from his embrace, distancing herself from him and reminding him that she was accustomed to sleeping alone.

He had wanted to talk, to forever vanquish the past, but she had interrupted him when he'd mentioned the baby and he'd understood that the subject was forbidden. The pain was behind them, never to be spoken of, never to be shared. He had known when they stood outside in the snow and she had said she loved him. There had been something in her expression, a shadowy secret in her eyes, and he had known. Oh, yes, he had known that this new commitment wasn't complete. Her lips had pleaded with him to stay, but her heart?

Be careful of the things you wish for, he thought ruefully. He had wished to have Amanda again and he had won, but the victory—if it could even be termed that—was oddly hollow. She loved him, he didn't doubt that, but for the first time he wasn't sure that loving was enough.

CHAPTER TEN

Her hand trembled. Amanda curled her fingers under until her nails pinched into her palm. The trembling stopped, then began again. She walked to the window, pulled back the draperies, let them fall into place.

I can't. I can't. I can't. The denial marched ceaselessly through her thoughts.

"Where are you, Dain?" she asked, her voice toneless in the silent house. He would be home at any moment. She longed to see him. She dreaded seeing him. *I can't. I can't.*

She made herself turn to the room, forced her concentration on the home she'd created for herself and Dain. Martha's rental house had become home when Dain had moved in; the rooms had taken on color and personality and Amanda had felt alive again. Dain had wanted to return to the house they'd planned and built together, but she had persuaded him to stay at the cottage. He had wanted to begin seeing friends they hadn't seen in months, but she had teasingly replied that this time together was private, like a second honeymoon. He had suggested she look for another job in her chosen field of interior design, but she had wanted to continue working at the child-care center for a while. She would be ready to move again in the spring, she had promised, and Dain had smiled that oddly sad smile.

And now spring was just a month away. How had the three months since Thanksgiving Day flown by so fast? Why hadn't she been more aware of the passing days, more conscious of the halcyon contentment she had known within these walls—within Dain's arms? Their relationship wasn't perfect, but it had grown from a tenuous trust to a steady acceptance. The uneasy silences had all but vanished between them and she had thought that spring would truly mean a new beginning—for herself, for Dain, and for their marriage.

A new beginning. Oh, God! I can't.

She stiffened at the sound of a car in the drive and her heart stopped. Beat, she told it. Beat. You can't stop now. Not now, when Dain would walk through the door at any second. Not when he would see her weak and shaking. No, she wouldn't let him see her that way. Beat, she commanded and felt it settle into an uneven rhythm as a car door slammed outside. Dain was home and Amanda wished he hadn't come.

Dain slammed the door of the Mercedes and glanced toward the house. Amanda would be waiting for him and the thought brought contentment with a discordant melody. She usually met him at the door with a kiss and a smile. Sometimes the smile was too determinedly cheerful and often the kiss was a little too intense, but he pretended not to notice.

It had become almost a game . . . the pretending, the

make-believe world they had created. A second honeymoon, Amanda was fond of saying, but he didn't share the analogy. It was more like probation, he thought, and then immediately stripped the word from his mind, knowing it wasn't fair. Amanda was trying to put everything in the proper balance; she was trying to make him happy. And he was happy. He only wished it didn't take so much effort.

He walked to the house, his briefcase knocking wearily against his leg. The door didn't swing open at his touch and as he reached into his pocket for the keys he wondered why it was locked. Amanda's car was parked in the drive, but he supposed she might have walked to Martha's. Still, it seemed odd. He shrugged aside the uneasy feeling and stepped inside the house. The hallway was dim and empty. Dain set his briefcase on the floor, his eyes seeking Amanda as he moved to the living room.

Relief flowed through him when he saw her standing by the window. Three months of being with her again should have eased the fear that it was only a dream, the sense of wonder that it was not. But each time he saw her, it was the same.

Her back was to him and she was staring out at the hazy February day through a narrow opening in the draperies. She seemed so small, so delicate, and his lips curved with tender pleasure. The black slacks she wore fit neatly, if a little loosely, over her legs and hips. A white lacy-weave sweater had just the right amount of cling to look elegantly tantalizing. Stylish waves of sable hair tumbled indiscreetly around her shoulders. It smelled of sunshine and a soft spring rain, a fragrance he knew by memory and that lingered in his mind whenever Amanda was near.

"I'm home." His greeting skimmed through the air,

sincere, symbolic, and he wondered if she had any idea of how much he loved her.

Amanda felt frozen, but from somewhere within herself she found the courage to turn and face him. In a dark suit he looked professional and distinguished. His hair was deeply gold and disarrayed by the wear and tear of a day's work. His brown eyes warmed her, made her want to run into the strength of his arms, but if he touched her, she would dissolve in an agony of tears and then he would know how very weak she was. She relaxed the tight clasp of her hands and thought that outwardly she must appear quite calm.

"Dain?" Her voice was raspy with nerves and she cleared her throat. "I'm pregnant."

Her words knocked the breath from him and his stomach winged to the floor only to jerk unsteadily into place again. Pregnant? A baby? *A baby!* Suddenly, he wanted to catch Amanda in his arms and whirl around the room with her, yelling and laughing with excitement. But he saw the wide sapphire eyes watching him and the joyous excitement gave way to concern. Amanda. She must be remembering and feeling very uncertain. He opened his mouth to ask if she was all right, but she stole the words from him.

"The doctor said I'm in good health. Everything should be fine." She paused, thinking that she'd been told that once before. But everything hadn't been fine. The crushing fear inside her grew larger, pushing the air from her lungs in quick, sharp stabs. "I didn't have any idea, Dain. I walked into his office believing I was just having the same old problems with my cycle and he told me—" A mirthless laugh cut off the words and she half-turned away from Dain's probing gaze. "He wanted to know what method

181

of birth control we'd been using and I laughed. Laughed! And then I told him how hard it had been for me to conceive the first time and that it just wasn't possible. I couldn't have gotten pregnant so easily this time. There had to be a mistake."

Dain took a tentative step toward her. "But there's no mistake? The doctor's sure?"

Amanda closed her eyes as the fear engulfed her. The nightmare was beginning again. "Yes," she whispered. "Yes, he's sure. Yes, I'm sure." *Yes, yes, yes. I can't. I can't. I can't.*

"Amanda," Dain said gently, comfortingly, "it will be all right this time, you'll see. Everything will be all right."

Blue eyes fastened on him with undisguised panic. "How do you know that? How can you possibly know that, Dain? It's starting again. I know it is and I can't go through with it. Do you hear me, Dain? I won't do it. I can't. I can't."

She was distraught by her fear. He could see it in her eyes, hear it in her voice, but he felt strangely distanced from her emotion. If she had come to him, made an effort to share her feelings or simply sought comfort in his arms, he would have soothed her, loved her. But she stood apart from him, rejecting him by the very distance she kept between them. Three months hadn't made a dent in that wall around her heart.

Amanda watched him, seeking to interpret the cool self-control that shuttered his thoughts from her. Was he afraid or indifferent? Resentful? Oh, no. She couldn't live through that again. "I know you don't want children, Dain. I know you resented my longing to have—"

"Resented? Our baby?" His fist clenched in alarm. "Are you out of your mind, Amanda? How could you believe such a thing of me? Do you think I'm so shallow I'd resent a child? God!" He pressed his palm to his forehead, hardly aware that he did so.

Confusion wrapped around her memories, clouding the facts in her mind. "But you never wanted to—to touch me or make love when . . ."

Dain shook his head slowly from side to side. "Sex by appointment is not my idea of making love. Two years of charts and gauging success or failure at the end of each month is frustrating, but I never resented it. Didn't you know how much I wanted a baby? Didn't I tell you?"

"You didn't act like it, Dain," she defended herself. "You didn't stay home long enough to convince me you meant anything you said." She saw the flicker of guilty concession in his eyes, and held her ground.

"What in hell was I supposed to do?" he asked. "You were unpredictable and moody. I honestly thought you were happier when I wasn't around. And besides, while you were decorating the nursery I was planning for the future. I felt I had to work harder to make that future possible for our child. Damn it, why am I telling you this now?" He jerked at the knot in his tie, loosened it, and pulled it off. Tossing it onto a chair, he removed his jacket and attempted to calm his thundering heartbeat.

"Why didn't you tell me then?" Amanda tried to sort through this new reality and free truth from the lie she'd believed.

"Why didn't you ask?" He pinned her with a probing stare. "You could have—what difference does it make, Amanda? We made mistakes and God knows we paid for them, but we won't make the same ones again. Not this time."

"No." The fear crawled down her back. This time. It

was going to happen again. No matter how wrong she'd been before or how many mistakes she'd made, she knew Dain could never understand the desperation she felt right now. There were some things a man couldn't possibly understand and some things she just didn't have the strength to face. "I can't go through with it, Dain. I can't."

Her pain wound its way through him, twisting and tearing at him until he knew it must be stopped. Did she think he was a stranger to fear? That he offered reassurance as a token for her sake alone? He wanted to give her the strength she needed, but still she kept the distance between them.

The anger began slowly as he faced her, but it built rapidly to a chilling fire. "You can't? What does that mean, Amanda? You are pregnant. Nothing is going to change that fact. Unless, you—" He couldn't finish the thought, much less the sentence.

The cold logic of his words washed over her and Amanda bowed her head, appalled at the idea of ever, in any way, harming the new life within her. From the moment she'd heard the incredible, unbelievable fact of conception, she had allowed the past to dictate her reaction. She hadn't thought of the alternative; she'd known only she couldn't survive another long and torturous tragedy. Her hand crept quietly, protectively, to her stomach and like a glimpse of light in a dense fog she realized what Dain must think of her. She lifted her gaze to his face and felt the white-hot heat of his anger scorch her.

"You're a fool, Amanda, if you think, for one second, I'd allow you to terminate this pregnancy." His voice faltered, then steadied. "I don't give a damn about what you think you can't do. You're so wrapped up in self-pity

184

that you're not capable of loving anyone but yourself. Right now you're certainly not demonstrating any love for our unborn child. And don't tell me you're afraid of what might happen. Everyone's afraid, Amanda. Even me. But you can't see that. All you can see is the past. You can't forget the past.

"Well, you're not going to blame me because you can't cope with life, not this time." Dain consciously slowed the rapid rise and fall of his chest as he stared dispassionately at Amanda's pale face. Her eyes seemed huge and misted with a sense of betrayal, but he hardened his heart against the sympathetic tug. Damn! He'd sheltered her long enough—that was his mistake—but he couldn't do it anymore.

"I've tried to understand. Tried to be patient with you and give you time to come to grips with your emotion, but I don't have any patience left, Amanda. When I came back from overseas, I wanted—needed—to comfort you, but you turned from me at every opportunity. So I told myself it was the circumstances; you couldn't think of anyone except our child. I could accept that, but then he died and you rejected my need to share that grief with you. I wanted to hold you, to give you my strength and to draw strength from you, but you didn't need me." His voice was low, but still thick with anger. "The night he died, I was so empty, so completely devastated, but all of my emotions seemed insignificant when I thought of you and how I had to help you survive the loss of our son."

Dain altered his stance, turned away from her, turned back. "I was so concerned for you, Amanda. And do you know what you said? 'It should have been me. I should have died too.'" His hand brushed at his hair, then jammed down into his pocket in barren remembrance.

"Do you know what that did to me, Amanda? Have you even once considered how I felt or that I hurt every bit as much as you did? Damn you, Amanda. I'm tired of fighting you and I'm tired of fighting for you. Everyone is entitled to his own private hell, so don't expect me to share yours any longer. I've found my own." He pivoted from the lost expression on her face and walked from the house, slamming the door behind him with loud finality.

The sound of his leaving echoed through the empty house just as his words echoed violently through her mind, shattering the wall of protection around her heart in one blow. With rapid-fire clarity his accusations seared the truth into her soul.

Dear God! How could she have been so blind? So insensitive? So utterly selfish? She hadn't considered him at all. Since she had carried the baby in her womb and given birth, she had believed that Dain's feelings were less important, less intense, than her own. And he had needed her, wanted the comfort she could give, but she had shut him out because she'd thought he couldn't understand, couldn't share her grief. She had withdrawn from him at the first sign of pain and, in doing that, she had selfishly denied them both a vital part of loving.

Oh, Dain. I'm sorry. It was such a hollow apology. It meant nothing. Nothing. He had left. . . .

A sob rose in her throat and fear took on a totally different meaning. Dain had left and she—oh, God, she had to stop him. She ran after him, knowing she couldn't let him leave. Not now. Not ever.

Jerking open the front door, she rushed onto the porch and her heart plunged to a halt when she saw Dain standing before her. His hand was closed around the wooden post and his back was to her. He stiffened at the sound of her appearance.

"This is as far as I could go," he stated scornfully. "Where you're concerned, I don't seem to have the courage of my convictions. I love you, Amanda. I don't know how such simple words can convey all I feel for you. How can saying I love you reveal the emptiness, the total nothing I am without you. How can it describe the inanity of just waking up alone? I wish I could walk away without a backward glance. I wish I could hate you, turn this futile needing and longing and yearning for you into hatred. But I don't even have the strength to do that. I don't have any fight left, Amanda. I love you." His jaw clenched in agonizing control and his voice faltered into a heart-rending whisper. "I just—love you."

In her whole life Amanda had never felt so humble, so completely unworthy. While she had been searching for a way to apologize for the unforgivable, he had forgiven her. From a heart that loved beyond her comprehension, he'd forgiven her. A solitary tear formed on her lashes and slipped onto her cheek, lingering there in helpless humility. "Don't leave me, Dain," she pleaded softly. "Please, I want this baby—your baby, but more than that I want you. I need you. Now and forever."

He turned. His eyes were liquid dark as he stared at the teardrop on her cheek and then gently lifted its shimmering wetness onto his fingertip. His face blurred as another teardrop replaced the first and was quickly followed by another and another. Amanda raised her hand in mute offering. "Until just now I didn't know what loving really meant. But I love you, Dain. I don't know how I can ever show you, but—" The tears bunched and clogged in her throat and she gave in to their healing river.

With a sigh Dain pulled her into his arms, quietly glad that he was there to hold her. Cry, Amanda, he told her in his heart. Cry. Feel again. Love again. Cry. And when you're through, I'll still be here, holding you, loving you. Always loving you.

When the tears dwindled to a mist, she pressed a kiss to his dampened shirt and looked into his eyes, eyes that were as moist as her own. Amanda felt her love swell as the wall around her heart dissolved forever and she committed herself to him without reservation. "The past can't hurt us anymore, Dain. Nothing will separate us again. I won't allow it. I'll fight to keep you close to me. You'll have to share my fears during these next few months, because I can't face them without you."

His hand stroked her face. "Everything will be all right with this baby, Amanda. It has to be—but whatever comes, we'll share it, good or bad, happiness or sorrow. Promise me that you'll share it with me, Amanda."

"I promise, Dain." No matter what happened, as long as she had his love, everything would be all right. It was almost spring. A time of new life, new beginnings. "Dain," she whispered. "I think it's time to go home."

His smile was like the rainbow after the storm. "Don't you know that in my arms you're already there?"

"Home," she whispered in soft, sweet contentment. "Forever."

As Dain bent to seal her vow with his lips, the promise drifted upward to catch on the wind like a benediction, sacred and enduring . . . forever.

All-new Candlelight Newsletter

An exceptional, *free* offer awaits readers of Dell's incomparable Candlelight Ecstasy and Supreme Romances.

Subscribe to our all-new CANDLELIGHT NEWSLETTER and you will receive—at absolutely no cost to you—exciting, exclusive information about today's finest romance novels and novelists. You'll be part of a select group to receive sneak previews of upcoming Candlelight Romances, well in advance of publication.

You'll also go behind the scenes to "meet" our Ecstasy and Supreme authors, learning firsthand where they get their ideas and how they made it to the top. News of author appearances and events will be detailed, as well. And contributions from the Candlelight editor will give you the inside scoop on how she makes her decisions about what to publish—and how *you* can try your hand at writing an Ecstasy or Supreme.

You'll find all this and more in Dell's CANDLELIGHT NEWSLETTER. And best of all, *it costs you nothing.* That's right! It's Dell's way of thanking our loyal Candlelight readers and of adding another dimension to your reading enjoyment.

Just fill out the coupon below, return it to us, and look forward to receiving the first of many CANDLELIGHT NEWSLETTERS—overflowing with the kind of excitement that only enhances our romances!

Candlelight Ecstasy Romances™

$1.95 each

At your local bookstore or use this handy coupon for ordering:

DELL READERS SERVICE— Dept. A108
P.O. BOX 1000, PINE BROOK, N.J. 07058-1000   B291C

Please send me the above title(s). I am enclosing $_____ (please add 75¢ per copy to cover postage and handling.) Send check or money order—no cash or COD.s. Please allow up to 8 weeks for shipment.

Name_____

Address_____

City_____ State/Zip_____